ESCAPE!

Clay Taggart ran a palm over his right shoulder and wished he was able to understand the Apache. For all he knew they might be discussing how to dispose of him. The pair by the spring hadn't stopped glaring at him from the moment he'd seen them. He suspected that if he turned his back on them at the wrong time, he'd end up with steel between his shoulders.

Clay glanced at the opening and debated whether to make a run for it. Every moment spent with the Apaches was another moment he cheated death. And no man's luck lasted forever. Grunting, he moved to the pool and splashed more water on his aching shoulders and back. The chilling stares of the nearby Apaches added to the goose flesh that broke out all over him.

Be patient, Clay told himself. He'd get his chance. Sooner or later, he would escape, and if the Apaches tried to stop him, he'd sell his life dearly.

1

WHITE APACHE

HANGMAN'S KNOT

Jake McMasters

LEISURE BOOKS NEW YORK CITY

To Judy, Joshua, and Shane.

A LEISURE BOOK®

November 1993

Published by

Dorchester Publishing Co., Inc.
276 Fifth Avenue
New York, NY 10001

Printed in the United States of America.

Chapter One

Clay Taggart knew he was a goner when his sorrel went lame. He was cresting a low ridge, his left arm raised to wipe the sweat from his burning brow, when the horse stumbled, recovered, and stumbled again. Reining up, Clay quickly dismounted and squatted beside its front legs. What he saw brought a lump to his throat.

"Damn my luck all to hell!" Clay angrily snapped. Gingerly, he reached out and touched the animal's swollen ankle, causing the sorrel to nicker and fidget.

A tiny tendril of dust rising from the arid plain Clay had just crossed caught his attention. He stood and glared at the dust a moment, then at the stretch of sunbaked landscape ahead of him. Arizona in the middle of summer was brutally hot, and only a fool or a wanted man would be abroad in such blistering heat. Clay was no fool. "I reckon I'm pretty near the end of my rope," he said in disgust. "I just wish I could have taken that bastard Gillett with me."

Working rapidly, Clay stripped off his saddle and saddle blanket. Both were placed in the shade of a nearby cactus. Then, rifle in hand, he returned to his horse and gave the animal a last pat on the neck. "I'm sorry, old fella. This needs to be done quietly." He drew his Bowie knife.

The sorrel looked at him dumbly, not understanding, and it was still gazing dumbly when a burning sensation lanced its neck and its blood gushed out over the packed earth.

"That's one more I owe Gillett," Clay said presently, moving aside as the animal tottered, then collapsed and thrashed wildly. He retrieved his saddlebags and his half-empty canteen, squared his broad shoulders, and hiked down the rise and out across the flat beyond. His face flushed red, but not from the scorching temperature. Rather, Clay Taggart turned red with rage at the thought of being caught before he could take revenge on the man responsible for his flight. "All I want is a chance to get even," he said to himself. "Just one chance."

In the distance reared hazy peaks, the Dragoon Mountains. Clay trudged toward them, heedless of the rivers of perspiration soaking his shirt and pants and of the constant pain in his feet. His high-heeled boots were so uncomfortable he debated taking them off, but decided against it when he realized doing so would slow him down even more. He knew reaching the mountains was hopeless, but they were the only hope he had, and like a drowning man he clung to the illusion in desperation.

Miles to the rear, the column of smoke grew thicker and thicker.

Other eyes saw it too, but from much closer. Dark, thoughtful eyes set in a swarthy face atop a powerfully built, stocky body. Cuchillo Negro lay behind a bush scarcely big enough to hide a cat and observed the dozen hated white-eyes 20 yards to the south. He easily could have picked off two or three before they knew what was happening, but he didn't. To alert them to his presence would be to alert them to the fact there was a band of Chiricahuas in the area, and no one must know that. So he contented himself with watching.

Seconds later the entire party halted at the command of a tall man sporting a shiny circle of metal on his vest. Cuchillo Negro noted with interest that this one was the apparent leader of the group. At a word from the tall one, another man, a Mexican in a wide sombrero, climbed down and closely examined the ground. After a bit the Mexican looked up and spoke in Spanish, a language Cuchillo Negro understood.

"He is less than two hours ahead of us, *señor*."

"Then we are gaining," said the leader.

"*Sí*, Marshal Crane."

"Climb up. I aim to hang that son of a bitch before nightfall, and nothing is going to stand in my way."

Hoofs thundering, the 12 hard men headed toward a far-off ridge. They deliberately held their mounts to a brisk walk, as any wise horsemen would do to conserve the strength of their animals during the worst part of the day.

Cuchillo Negro waited until the whites were swallowed by the dust they made. Then he rose, turned, and trotted to the northeast, moving at a pace that would have astounded the men he had just seen. His bronzed muscles rippling, he covered two miles in half the time it would have taken them, and once among the hills he stuck to narrow game trails winding through the thickest of brush, until at length he came to a wide hollow where a small spring shimmered in the sunshine and dozens of his people milled among scattered wickiups. He went straight to several warriors seated near the spring, and addressed one whose commanding features and size marked him as a person of distinction. "*Inday pindah lickoyee.*"

"How many?"

"*Nah-kee-sah-tah.*"

"Are they after us?"

"No, Delgadito. They chase another white-eye."

"Whites chasing a white? Why would they do such a thing?"

Cuchillo Negro remembered the comment he had heard. "They want to hang him."

One of the listeners, a small, wiry warrior named Chiquito, snorted. "This is new to me. Hang him how? Upside down from a tree?"

"I do not know," Cuchillo Negro admitted.

"I know," Delgadito said, rising. He idly placed a hand on the cartridge belt looped around his muscular waist. "When we were on the reservation, the agent told me how they punish those of their kind who kill others of their kind." Glancing about, he spotted the object he desired and went over to pick it up. "They take this," he said, hefting the rope he held, "wrap it around the neck, and hang the guilty ones."

Chiquito scrunched up his face. "Only the whites would take life in such a strange manner."

"Where is the honor in such a death?" wondered Amarillo. "Why do they not let a challenge settle the matter?"

"The whites are too strange for any man to understand," Chiquito said, voicing an opinion common among their people. "And what they do is of no interest to me."

"It is a wise man who learns all he can of his enemies," Delgadito said.

At that moment, well to the southeast of the hollow, Clay Taggart had his own enemy very much in mind as he trudged woodenly through a virtual inferno toward the cool, beckoning heights of the Dragoon Mountains. Long since had he discarded the empty canteen and his saddlebags, keeping only a box of ammunition which he had crammed into a pocket. He was so hot his skin seemed on fire and his lungs seared with each step he took. Yet he refused to quit. Giving up wasn't in the Taggart nature. Never had been. Back in South Carolina, before the war, the Taggart clan had been known for their grit and determination. As the last of the line he had a family tradition to uphold.

Clay blinked sweat from his eyes and licked his dry lips. He figured he had been walking for three hours, perhaps four, and he was mildly surprised the posse hadn't overtaken him. Soon they would, though. He hoped he had enough energy left to give them a decent fight. After all that had happened, the shame would be more than he could bear if he let them take him without making them pay dearly.

"Gillett," Clay hissed, letting his hatred lend stamina to his limbs. "You stinking, rotten . . ." He broke off. Words failed him. There were none to describe a human vulture so unbelievably wicked, so downright evil. Clay halted, overcome by the intensity of his feelings. And as he stood there quietly he heard something that jerked his head up and made his pulse race faster. He heard the clomp of a hoof.

Clay wheeled, leveling the Winchester as he did. He was unable to hide his astonishment at seeing 12 riders strung out in a long line, the nearest not ten yards away. Their smirking faces told him they had been there for quite some time. They had been dogging his heels for miles, yet he had been too befuddled by the heat to realize it! At their center rode Tom Crane, and at sight of him Clay worked the lever of his rifle and croaked, "You polecat! You're not taking me back!"

Oddly, Crane made no move to defend himself. His grin widened, nothing more.

Clay heard a slight swishing sound. Having been a rancher for years, he knew what it was, and looked up just as the rope settled over his shoulders. With a hard jerk he was yanked off his feet. He winced as his right side felt the impact, which jarred the Winchester from his grasp. The rope bit into his shirt, into his skin, and then he was being propelled across the flat as if shot from an 18-pounder. Cactus bit into his face, his body. Sharps limbs tore at his flesh. He struggled mightily, but failed to loosen the rope.

Men were galloping to keep up on both sides, most cackling crazily at the expense of the man they had trailed for so long. "Tell me, Taggart!" a bearded rider taunted. "Was she worth it?"

Clay wanted to strangle the man with his bare hands, but he was helpless to do more than grit his teeth, close his eyes, and pray to high heaven he survived the ordeal. His midsection slammed into something hard, and he thought for a moment he had been ripped open by a sharp rock. A hasty glance revealed only a tear in his shirt and a jagged gash in his stomach.

The rider who had roped Clay whooped wildly and waved his hat as he galloped steadily eastward. Twice he looked back, showing youthful features distinguished by pudgy cheeks.

I'll get you too! Clay fumed. *If it's the last thing I ever do!* To his way of thinking they were all as guilty as Gillett. Most of them knew how Gillett treated her, knew the circumstances of her marriage. Yet they did nothing to help her. So they deserved the same fate as the man they had sided with.

Suddenly Clay saw a barrel cactus directly in his path. Frantically he twisted sharply to the left, but he wasn't quick enough. Like a bat going out of hell he smacked into the cactus head-first. Intense agony contorted his face as the needles bit deep. He felt his body slide over the obstacle, felt torment such as he had never known.

All around him the men laughed harder.

Clay sagged, weakening more and more by the moment. Blood was flowing over his chin and the front of his shirt was sticky. He didn't know how badly he had been hurt, but it was bad enough. When they brought him before Gillett he'd be unable to stand, a mockery of a man. And she would see him.

Fresh fury fanned Clay into making a futile effort to slip free of the rope. Wriggling and straining, he tried his utmost, and failed. The circulation had been cut off for so long his arms were going numb and he couldn't get the leverage he needed. His steely muscles had been rendered useless. The heat and the punishment had reduced him to a shell of his former self.

Clay dimly realized he had been dragged for a long time, and the young rider showed no signs of slowing. He wondered if they aimed to drag him to death, then decided against the notion. Gillett would want him alive. But as the seconds became minutes and the minutes went on he began to have his doubts. His clothes were being gradually torn from his body. He was being battered and bruised and cut with every yard he traveled.

"Don't wear your horse out over this trash, Santee!" someone yelled.

"Yeah," chimed in another. "Let some of us take turns! You can't have all the fun."

Bitter bile rose in Clay's throat. Being so powerless was almost more than he could bear. The humiliation was so overpowering he bit his lip to keep from raging mindlessly at his attackers. Inwardly, his pride stung worse than his wounds. But that had always been the way. Some would say that his pride had always been his great weakness, the flaw in his character that had gotten him into more trouble than anything else.

A patch of thick brush appeared. Clay braced himself, tucking his head into his shoulders, but no amount of tensing could prepare him for the excruciating agony of being slashed to ribbons by slender, razor-sharp branches. He tasted blood on his tongue and spat it out. Summoning the meager reserves of vitality that remained to him, he moved his left hand, trying to find the hilt of his Bowie. It was doubtful he could draw the knife and saw through the rope, but he had to try. The sheath, however, was all he found; the knife had been knocked loose somewhere.

Dizziness set in, causing the world to spin insanely. Clay bit his lip and tried resisting the dark, swirling tide, but it was like trying to resist a gigantic whirlpool. He was sucked into the midst of an abyss, losing all sensation.

Was it minutes or hours later that Clay was jolted to partial wakefulness by a cold sensation on his face? Reviving was akin to climbing a tall ladder; he could see a bright spot of light at the top of the ladder, but the light stayed the same no matter how high he climbed. He was getting no closer to it when the light abruptly swooped down upon him and there he was, lying on his back on rocky ground and blinking at the dazzling sun, his face soaking wet from the water that had been splashed on him.

"Finally," someone muttered. "Let's get this over with. I have me a mare about to deliver."

"Keep your britches on, Prost. We have to do this right, no matter how long it takes."

The speakers Clay recognized. The first was Jacob Prost, a small rancher who lived southeast of Tuscon. The other was Marshal Tom Crane.

"You should let us use this varmint for target practice, Marshal," suggested someone behind Clay. "The buzzards will take care of the rest."

"And what if an old prospector or someone else should happen to stumble on the body, Santee?" Crane responded. "There would be talk, and maybe word would get back to the federal law." He shook his head. "No, we do this the way Mr. Gillett wants, all nice and legal."

"I've always wanted to attend a necktie social," another man remarked, which met with widespread snickers.

The full meaning of the words slowly dawned on Clay. He tried to sit up, and got to his elbows when another bout of weakness flattened him. "You can't," he rasped. "It isn't right."

"What the hell would you know about right and wrong?" Marshal Crane declared, bending down. "Any *hombre* who would force himself on another man's wife is the lowest vermin there is. Even worse than Apaches."

"I did not!" Anger brought Clay to a sitting posture. "Lilly and I have been—" His statement was viciously ended by a fist to the jaw that stretched him out on the rocks.

"None of us care to hear your lies, Taggart," Marshal Crane said. "Truth speaks louder than words."

"Want me to fetch the rope?" Santee asked eagerly.

"Do it," Crane said.

Clay resisted more dizziness. His life was at stake, and unless he did something and did it fast he would never see Lilly again, never know the sweet scent of her hair or the lush contours of her full body against his. None of the posse were paying much attention to him; they all considered him too far gone to be much of a threat. But he was a Taggart and Taggarts just didn't die so easily. He saw a pair of legs to his left, then a tract of trees and undergrowth. If he could gain cover, he might be able to save his hide yet.

"I will say one thing for this scum," the high-pitched voice of Jack Bitmer remarked. "He led us on a fine chase. Another day and my horse would have been worn to a frazzle."

"Taggart's running days are over," Marshal Crane said testily.

Not if Clay could help it. Composing himself, he bunched his muscles, ignored the piercing anguish doing so provoked, and rolled to the right, into the legs of the man at his side. A startled yelp, fingers clutching at his leg, and then he was up and in the clear, racing for the sanctuary the undergrowth promised. A single shot shattered the air, the slug punching into the earth at his feet.

"Don't shoot, damn you!" Marshal Crane roared.

An instant later Clay plunged into the vegetation, crouched, and slanted to the left. He could hear the lawman continue to bellow.

"Vasquez, take four men and go bring him back! And be quick about it!"

Clay glanced skyward, trying to get his bearings. The sun was to his left, almost to the horizon, so he was heading to the northeast. He saw a ragged peak to the left, and was shocked to realize the posse had brought him to the western edge of the Dragoon

Mountains. The presence of scattered cottonwoods and willow trees told him why; they needed a limb for the rope.

"This way, *amigos!*"

Diving into a thicket, Clay crawled though it to the far side and stood. He knew of Vasquez, knew the Mexican was a canny tracker, the best in the territory, which was why Vasquez was on Gillett's payroll. He had to find hard ground, so hard he wouldn't leave footprints, or Vasquez would be on him like a human bloodhound. Changing directions, he ran to the right, skirted a boulder, and nearly slipped down the bank of a narrow stream.

Here was a godsend if ever Clay saw one. Entering the water, he followed it eastward, staying in the middle where a layer of pebbles was firm enough to stand on without leaving tracks. He ran, or tried to, but his abused body was tiring and his veins seemed filled with lead. Puffing and huffing, he went around a bend and paused to take a few deep breaths. *He couldn't quit now!* Not after all he had been through, not after the punishment he had taken.

Clay shuffled onward, aware his clothes were hanging in tatters, aware he was covered with dried blood, welts, and bruises. Scores of cactus needles were imbedded in his flesh and one eye was partially swollen shut. He wanted to curl up and sleep for a week, but he dared not rest, not until he was safe.

Of a sudden Clay felt a prickling at the nape of his neck, a sure sign he was being watched. Thinking Vasquez had caught him, he turned, but the gurgling stream and barren banks teased him with their emptiness. There was no one there, nor could he hear anyone close at hand. Mystified, he lurched into a clumsy trot, moving his limbs by sheer force of will.

Clay had covered 40 yards when a cluster of boulders on a slope offered a temporary haven. By now he could hardly lift a finger, let alone a leg. So scrambling up over the knee-high bank, he tottered to the boulders, slipped between two of them, and gratefully sank to his knees on bare earth. He gasped for air and winced at spasms in his stomach. Just when he thought he had snatched triumph from defeat, his own body betrayed him. "Damn you!" he whispered, and punched his own leg.

Clay thought of Lilly, and those awful moments after Gillett burst in on them. He remembered the hurt in her eyes when Gillett called her a whore, and once again he felt molten lava course through him as he imagined burying his Bowie into Gillett again and again and again.

A shadow fell over the crack between the boulders.

Glancing up, Clay wanted to scream in rage when he laid eyes on the sneering face of Sergio Vasquez. He gripped a handful of loose dirt and flung it at the tracker as the Mexican came at him, but all Vasquez did was laugh. From behind strong arms seized him. He was hoisted to his feet.

"A good try, *señor*," Vasquez said, and made a clucking sound. "Walking in water does not leave many tracks, but it does stir up mud. You should keep that in mind if you ever have to track someone."

The men holding Clay chortled. Clay strained against them, to no avail. He looked, and recognized Art Jacoby and Bill Hesket. "Boys," he said, mustering a lopsided grin. "It's me. Your old pard, Clay. Let me go and no one will ever be the wiser."

"We can't do that and you know it," Jacoby replied.

"Gillett would ruin us," Hesket added.

"But we were pards. We've played cards on more Saturday nights than I can count. We've gotten drunk together," Clay said, trying to appeal to the friendship they had once shared. "That should count for something."

"It does." Hesket nodded. "It means we'll see that they make it quick and painless."

"I'll check the knot myself to be sure they do it right," Jacoby said. "You'll have a quick finish, I promise you. No dangling and strangling for minutes on end."

"You back-stabbing sons of bitches," Clay snarled. He was shoved into the open, hauled to the bank, and practically dragged back to where the rest were waiting. In his absence a horse had been positioned under a sturdy limb on a weeping willow and a rope had been tied above the saddle.

"Enjoy your exercise?" Marshal Crane taunted.

"Go to hell!" Clay responded.

"You first, Taggart."

Crane nodded, and two other men advanced to take Clay to the bay. Clay fought the best he could, but was unable to resist being bound at the wrist and lifted into the saddle. Tears of wrath filled his eyes and he had to blink again to clear them.

"Look at 'im!" someone exclaimed. "The fool is cryin' like a baby."

Clay twisted so he could stare at each and every one of the 12. He knew them all, either by name or by sight, and he branded their features into his memory. For what they had done, for what they were about to do, he owed them the same debt he owed Miles Gillett. Not that remembering them would do him much good. He would never have the chance to repay them for their vile deed.

"Get the rope on him," Crane directed.

Several men held Clay still as Santee rode along-side and draped the noose around his neck. The young gunman was enjoying himself immense-ly. "Try not to drool all over yourself," he said, beaming.

Art Jacoby, true to his word, inspected the knot, then faced Marshal Crane. "All set. Just give the word."

"About time." The lawman locked eyes with Clay. "If it was anyone but you, I'd offer a smoke or a bite to eat or even some coffee. But I never have liked you much, you smug bastard. So *adios*." His arm flew up, then down.

Clay heard a hand slap the rump of the bay and the horse leaped forward.

Chapter Two

At the moment the horse lunged into motion, Clay Taggart instinctively clamped his legs on the animal's sweaty sides, but holding fast was impossible. The bay galloped out from under him and Clay felt himself falling. He didn't fall far, not more than three of four inches, when he was brought up short at the end of the rope. The noose constricted, digging into his skin, into his throat, into his windpipe.

Clay sucked in air as his body dropped to its full length. He grimaced when the noose gouged in deep and for a second he thought his neck would snap. Some members of the posse were laughing, others were already riding off. He barely noticed. All he could think of, the only thing that mattered, was staying alive a few more precious seconds. Involuntarily he kicked, then promptly stopped when the movement made the rope tighten even further. As if from a great distance he heard a muffled voice.

"So much for the tough man! I don't see why Gillett was so worried. Come on, boys. Let's light a shuck!"

Dimly, Clay registered the drumming of hoofs. He saw swirls of fine dust hovering before him. His chest ached terribly as the rope twisted, swinging him from right to left. The posse was heading out across the flat. Only one rider, Santee, bothered to look back, and he grinned devilishly before vanishing into a dust cloud. Clay's right forefinger twitched, as if he was pulling a trigger.

How much time had gone by? Clay tried to make the air in his lungs last, but there were limits to how much the human body could endure. His misery intensified. He felt his lungs were close to bursting. Greedily he opened his mouth and attempted to breathe, to force fresh air past the horrible constriction in his throat. The effort was useless. His consciousness began to dim, his eyelids to flutter.

And as Taggart's eyes closed, other sets of eyes observed him from the cover of the nearby brush, dark eyes that betrayed no hint of emotion except for a single pair. Delgadito looked on and nodded, impressed by what he had seen. He glanced at the departing whites, all of whom were now shrouded by dust, and then at Cuchillo Negro and Amarillo. "Cut him down."

Soundlessly the pair of stout warriors obeyed. Cuchillo Negro, the younger of the two, went up the tree in a flash. A knife gleamed in the sunlight. Amarillo, waiting below, caught hold of the limp white man, letting the man slump over his shoulder, and then sprinted for the undergrowth. The body was much heavier than he had expected and he grunted from the weight. He was bending over to avoid a branch when his right foot caught in an exposed

root and he tripped, falling onto his right knee. As
he did, the body of the white man whipped forward,
thudding onto the ground, and Amarillo, unable to
check his momentum, fell onto the body, onto the
man's stomach. He thought the white-eye was dead,
so he was more than a little surprised when the man
coughed and spluttered and convulsed.

Suddenly Delgadito was there. The tall warrior
crouched, his brawny hands tugging at the rope
around the white man's throat, loosening the noose
a fraction at a time. Loud gasps came from the white
man and his eyelids trembled but did not open. At
length he lay still, breathing deeply but raggedly.

"What do we do with him?" Amarillo asked, touching the shredded remains of the man's pants. "He has
nothing worth stealing."

"We take him to our *kunh-gan-hay*."

Amarillo glanced up, puzzled. He was tempted to
question the wisdom of such a move, but he did not.
Too many times had Delgadito proven to be a master
at *na-tse-kes*, at the deep thinking that brought so
many rewards to himself and his band, for Amarillo
to object. "It will be as you want."

Four warriors, Delgadito among them, lifted the
white man and bore him at a trot to the north along
the strip of sparse vegetation serving as the boundary
between the mountains and the flatland. Over a mile
they went, and then they turned westward, moving
with heightened caution because now they were out
in the open. El Chico ran on ahead to be sure there
were no nasty surprises waiting, while Pasqual fell to
the rear to keep an eye on their back trail. They dared
not let down their guard for a minute, not now when
their homeland crawled with their enemies. Eternal
vigilance was the price they paid for continued survival, and every man there had lost too many friends
or relatives to slack off for a moment.

As Delgadito ran, he thought. He had listened
with interest to the words of the whites, who were
so stupid they had not known anyone else was within
miles of them. He had seen with his own eyes how
the big man with the mane of brown hair had stood
up to them, had tried to escape, and then, when
recaptured, had not shown the slightest fear when
they had thrown him onto the horse and slipped
the rope over his neck. No, not this one! Delgadito
had seen nothing but hatred in the big man's gaze,
even when the man's eyes watered, and nothing but
a thirst for vengeance in the set of the big man's face.
And Delgadito had been impressed.

It was twilight when the band arrived at the hollow. The women had tiny fires going in front of
the wickiups and the small children were eagerly
waiting for their meager suppers. Some of the older
boys were tending the five remaining horses.

Delgadito looked and felt the need to cough. To
see his people reduced to this was enough to make
him gnash his teeth in misery, but he would not
give in to such weakness. No, he gave a word of
greeting to one of the older boys who was showing
promise, and smiled at a little girl, pretending that
all was well, that all was as it should be when he
knew, and everyone there knew, their people were
in dire need.

"Where do you want this smelly white thing?"
Chiquito inquired, turning his nose away from the
leg he held.

For an answer Delgadito pointed at the ground
near his wickiup, and the white man was deposited
none too gently. The other warriors drifted off.
Delgadito walked over to his wife, who was squatting
by the fire, skinning a rabbit. "Mend him," he said.

Delgadito bent low to enter the wickiup. Inside,
he stripped off his bow and quiver, and was leaning

them against the side when he sensed rather than heard her behind him. "You have something to say?"

"We heal our enemies now?"

"When it suits our purpose."

"Whites killed my father and my brother."

"Would I have forgotten?"

"Yet still you ask this of me?"

"No, *ish-tia-nay*. I *tell* you to do it," Delgadito said, and saw her back stiffen. She left quietly, properly put in her place. He went out and sat cross-legged, watching her take out her anger on the rabbit, which she hacked to pieces as if it was the white man instead. As the meat cooked she set out gourd dishes containing pinion nuts and wild onions.

Delgadito ate in silence while staring off into the distance. He knew there would be others like her, others who did not understand, who would object strongly. Chiquito for one. Fiero for another. He must convince them he was right and then hope he had not made a critical mistake, a blunder that could cost him the position of influence he had earned only after much self-denial and hardship.

From out of the darkness Pasqual appeared. "Two fires," he announced. "To the west and to the south."

"I would see," Delgadito said, rising. He padded to the top of the hollow where El Chico and Fiero were standing and peered at the bright points of light. The fire to the west had to be that of the men responsible for the hanging. Only whites made their fires so big the flames could be seen for many miles. The one to the south was much smaller, although not as small as Indians would make.

"Mexicans?" El Chico said.

"Too far north of the border," Delgadito said, turning to go back. Neither party, in his opinion, posed a threat to his band, so he could devote his full attention to the matter of the white man. But he hadn't taken two strides when Fiero addressed him.

"I was out hunting when you brought the white dog to our camp."

Composing his features, Delgadito slowly faced the man who had caused him more trouble than all the other warriors combined. Fiero richly deserved his Spanish name; he had the temperament of a wildfire, and when aroused he was as fierce as an enraged mountain lion. Exceptionally strong and keen of eyesight, Fiero was the single best warrior besides Delgadito himself. And Fiero did not bother to hide the fact he would one day like to supplant Delgadito as the band's leader.

"When can we burn out his brains?" Fiero asked.

"The white man is not to be harmed," Delgadito said.

"Is it not enough his kind have stolen our land and forced most of our people onto the reservation? Are we Maricopas, that we jump to do their bidding whenever they so much as blink an eye?"

"This man did not ask for our help."

"Then why?"

"You will understand in time."

Fiero uttered a grunt of disgust. "I will never understand you, Delgadito. Whenever I think I am following your trail, you take another path and confuse me." He glowered at the larger fire to the west. "There is only one way to treat whites. We must kill them, kill them all, drive them from our homeland so the Shis-Inday can go back to the old ways, to the practices of our forefathers and their forefathers before them."

"There is no going back. The whites will never leave."

"Then we must make the land run red with their blood," Fiero declared, and El Chico murmured assent. "We must kill every one we find, including the dog you have brought here."

"There are too many and they are all over." Delgadito held his ground. "It is not like the old days when we could strike whenever and wherever we wanted. We must choose carefully and be miles away before the whites know what has happened."

"Are the Shis-Inday women?" Fiero asked in disgust.

Saying nothing, Delgadito started to turn. He should have known he would not get off so easily. Fiero threw a challenge at him.

"I am going to steal horses. What do you say to that?"

Delgadito did not want anyone to leave camp. It was true they had eaten almost all their horses, and were rationing the rest because game was very scarce. The bellies of the little ones and the women were rarely full any more. But he did not want to risk a warrior being captured, or even seen, because it would arouse suspicions and a search party might be sent out. Despite this, he dared not object. Warriors were free to do as they pleased, whenever they pleased. Reluctantly, he swallowed his budding anger and simply said, "We can always use more meat."

Fiero puffed up his chest and grinned at El Chico as if to say, "See? He does not dare refuse me." Unslinging his bow, he stated aloud, "I will be back by morning with enough horses for a grand feast." He took a step, then paused to regard both distant campfires. Presently he choose the smaller one and trotted southward.

El Chico leaned toward Delgadito. "I will go with him and make certain he comes back safely."

"If I owned a rifle, I would give it to you," Delgadito said in gratitude, for the giving of a rifle was akin to making a brother of a man selected to receive the gift. He watched the older warrior melt into the night, and walked down into the hollow with a heavy weight off his shoulders. El Chico was thoroughly dependable; he would keep Fiero in line.

About 40 yards to the south the object of Delgadito's concern had paused to adjust his knee-high moccasins to their full height as a protection against cactus. He heard the footfalls that no white man would have heard, and he was straightening up when El Chico ran up to him. "Did he send you to bring me back?"

"No," the older man said. "If you would have me, I would go with you."

"I travel fast," Fiero boasted, and proceeded to do so, breaking into a mile-eating trot as he headed out across the desert. He wasn't fooled for an instant. El Chico was a close friend of Delgadito's and had never expressed an interest in Fiero before. Yet Fiero did not refuse the request. Here was a chance to earn honor in the eyes of the others. If he was successful, he would have as his witness one of the closest friends of the man he so despised. Who better to vouch for his prowess before the whole band?

The pair of Chiricahuas flitted like ghosts across the murky landscape. There was no moon, yet they saw clearly. There were plenty of stones and rocks and occasional dry weeds in their path, yet they made no sound. They covered one mile, and then another, yet they breathed evenly, without any sign of having exerted themselves.

Fiero was in his element. He lived for the raid, for the slaying of his enemies and the stealing of whatever he could lay his hands on. His father had taught him both arts, and so much more. By the age of ten he had become expert with the bow and the knife. By the age of 12 he could run over five miles through the worst of country and be ready to run five more as soon as he was done. By the age of 15 he had killed his first man, a Mexican trader, and since then he had added dozens to his total. Fiero took great pride in his accomplishments and couldn't wait to add to them.

El Chico, on the other hand, was having second thoughts. He had offered to go along as a favor to Delgadito, but the further they went, the more he doubted the wisdom of his action. Several moons ago two other men had gone off with Fiero and only one had returned, which was why no one else had gone out with Fiero since. The loss of a life was a bad omen and did not reflect well on whoever led a raid. El Chico wished he had remembered that death and not been so hasty.

Gradually they neared the fire. Fiero hoped to find Mexican traders, since they were so ridiculously easy to slay. He would settle for smugglers, although they were more seasoned, more wary. And if the party turned out to be a family on its way from the northern provinces of Mexico to Tuscon, so much the better. Fiero had need of a wife, and he had long craved a Mexican beauty such as several other members of the band had. It was said Mexican women could drive a man crazy with their lovemaking and he was anxious to put the rumor to the test.

The camp had stupidly been made right out in the open. Evidently those sleeping by the fire believed no one could approach them without being seen by the lone guard.

Fiero halted 50 yards out and crouched. He saw cactus and weeds and mesquite all growing close to the camp and inwardly he smiled. The sombrero on the guard told him these were indeed Mexicans and his inner smile widened. On the south edge of the camp was a long string of horses.

Motioning to El Chico, Fiero moved in a crouch, circling the camp. When young, Fiero had been an apt pupil, learning his lessons well. And the first lesson he had learned about raiding an enemy was this: A warrior should never make a move until the number of his enemies has been determined, along with the number of their weapons and the goods they have worth stealing. The second lesson was related to the first: Any weakness an enemy has must be discovered so it can be exploited.

This camp had so many weaknesses there were almost too many for Fiero to believe. There was only the one guard; the guard was facing the fire, not out into the desert; there was cover close to the sleepers; there was no one watching the horses; and the horses had all been tethered to a single rope, making the job of stealing them a simple task.

Fiero made a slow, painstaking circuit of the entire camp, and when he was back at the point where he had started, he crouched. "There are enough horses to last us for weeks," he whispered.

"I do not like it," El Chico responded.

"Did you see something I did not? If they made it any easier for us, we could walk in and take what we want."

"Something bothers me," El Chico insisted.

Fiero wondered if this was part of a plan, if maybe Delgadito had asked El Chico to try and talk him out of going through with the raid. It would be like Delgadito to do such a thing. The man was as crafty as a fox, as devious as a white. "You can go back if you want. I will steal the horses by myself."

El Chico glanced at the camp. He could not say exactly why he was disturbed, but his every instinct warned him to pass this opportunity up.

"Well?" Fiero prompted.

Indecision made El Chico hesitate. If he left, and later Fiero returned with the horses, he would be shamed before all the others.

"I cannot wait all night."

"Very well," El Chico said.

"Here is how I want to do it," Fiero said. He went into detail, and when he was done he spun and circled once again to the south side of the camp. There he searched about until he found a small cluster of grass which he plucked and stuck into the top of his headband above his eyes. By arranging the stems across his brow and pulling them under the headband and down over his face to his mouth, leaving just enough space at the eyes to see clearly, he transformed his head into the very cluster of grass he had yanked out.

Flattening, Fiero set his bow and bobcat-hide quiver aside and began crawling toward the horses. He needed his hands free to grab hold of one and mount. Later, when the camp quieted down, he would return for the bow and none of the Mexicans would be any wiser.

There was a certain technique to the stalking crawl that Fiero's people had perfected during countless decades of practice. By keeping his arms tucked to his sides and using only his elbows and knees to move his body forward, he made it impossible for anyone to detect his movements. And by advancing a little at a time, he insured that anyone who happened to glance in his direction would see nothing but an innocent clump of grass swaying slightly in the cool northwesterly breeze.

Fiero had done this many times. He had stalked deer and antelope and gotten so close he could see their nostrils quivering when he loosed his arrows. He had stalked bears, and gotten so close he could have slapped them on the rump if he'd wanted. But the easiest of all to stalk were whites and Mexicans, who had the senses of a rock and the brains of a two-year-old. Often, like now, stalking them was no challenge at all. Just once Fiero would like to stalk a worthy foe, someone whose abilities were the equal of his own.

By now, Fiero knew, El Chico was stalking the camp from the north. El Chico would creep close enough to the guard to put an arrow into the man's back if the man so much as moved while Fiero was stealing the horses. If that happened, El Chico would then fade into the darkness while Fiero galloped off with the stock and the foolish Mexicans would be left to yell and jump up and down and waste their ammunition firing at empty air.

Fiero scanned the sleepers as he neared the string. There were nine in all, bundled in their blankets, and not a one had so much as twitched since first he'd laid eyes on them. He thought it a bit strange that the Mexicans were covered with blankets on such a warm night, since even whites and Mexicans were hardy enough to sleep in the open in the summer, but since the ways of his enemies were often mystifying, he did not think it so strange as to warrant much attention. And that was his undoing.

Fiero snaked ever closer, his steely muscles rippling, his right hand always close to the hilt of his large knife. He was 15 yards from the horses when he saw one the sleepers, or rather one of the *blankets*, move ever so slightly. An instant later the night was shattered by thunder, or what seemed to be thunder but was actually the simultaneous blasting of many guns.

Pain seared Fiero's brow. He felt moist blood on his face. Realizing that somehow he had been spotted, that the Mexicans were trying to kill him, he threw caution to the wind and, leaping up, he raced to the south. More rifles boomed. Slugs tore into the ground to the right and left. Fiero covered a mere ten yards when a black veil claimed his mind and he fell.

The shock of striking the hard ground snapped Fiero back to life. He heard shouts, heard rushing footsteps. Scrambling to his hands and knees, he angled to the left, blinking blood from his eyes. He could hardly see for more than a few feet. Suddenly the ground opened up under him and he slid down a short incline into a shallow dry wash, not more than hip-deep and only the width of his shoulders. But it was enough to temporarily hide him, and he lay still, on his back, listening to the thud of boots and the jingle of spurs. There were shouts in Spanish, which, like many of his people, he was somewhat familiar with, and shouts in English, which he recognized as being English even though he knew little of the language itself.

"Where did the *bastardo* go?" a Mexican roared.

"He vanished," said another.

"Keep looking!"

The search went on for a long time. Fiero expected them to find him at any moment, but they were concentrating on an area west of him. Finally one of them gave a shout and there was excited jabbering in Spanish. They had found his bow and quiver.

"He must have crawled off to die! He wouldn't leave these behind if he wasn't hurt badly," one said.

The voices and the footfalls retreated to the camp. Wincing from the effort, Fiero pushed himself to the top of the wash. He saw many men, Mexicans and whites alike, which amazed him. And then he saw El Chico being dragged in, El Chico wounded and doubled over in torment, and he felt his blood turn hot. One of the whites, a huge man sporting a long brown beard, stepped close to the fire. When Fiero saw the blue cap the man wore, and the curved sword the man drew as he grabbed hold of El Chico's hair, Fiero understood at last. He knew he must hurry to the hollow and warn his people, but as he turned to crawl off another black veil enveloped his mind and the last thing he remembered was his face smacking the dirt.

Chapter Three

Clay Taggart came awake slowly, clawing his way up through a gloomy fog that hemmed him in on every side, clawing and flailing until all of a sudden the fog broke and his eyes were open and he was staring up at the strangest roof he had ever beheld, a curious thatched affair made of reeds, grass, and brushwood. A stabbing pang in his throat reminded him of the hanging. He sat bolt upright, panic-stricken, and glanced around in confusion, trying to make sense of what he saw. There were bowls and baskets lined up against one side. Blankets were piled together. And near the entrance leaned a club of some sort. *A war club!* Clay realized, just as a shadow fell across the opening.

Into the dwelling came a middle-aged Indian woman clad in a buckskin dress, her long raven hair down past her shoulders, her dark eyes lighting with fear when she saw him.

33

"An Apache!" Clay blurted out. He glanced up. "I'm in a damn wickiup!" Stunned, he simply sat there as the woman moved to the bowls and fiddled with a small one. He could do no more than gape when she brought it over to him and indicated, by touching the rim to her lips, that he should drink the murky contents. "What the hell is going on?" Clay croaked, barely able to talk, his throat was so raw.

The entrance darkened again, and inside came a tall, superbly muscled warrior.

Clay's first reaction was to claw for his Colt, only his Colt wasn't there. Glancing down, he saw to his dismay that he was completely naked except for, of all things, an Apache breechcloth. He also saw scores of wounds dotting his body, the cuts and welts and gashes caused during his ordeal, and he idly wondered why they gave him no pain.

"Drink, white-eye."

Startled, Clay stared at the somber warrior, so typical of the hardy breed he had seen a few times before when he'd delivered cattle to the reservation: black hair bound at the forehead with a strip of cloth; a wide, smooth brow; piercing eyes; a hawk nose; and a tight, thin mouth that had probably never cracked in a grin. The warrior wore a long-sleeved shirt, a breechcloth, and high moccasins. At his waist hung a big knife. No other weapon was visible.

"You hear, *pindah lickoyee?*"

Clay dumbly nodded. *Pindah lickoyee* was Apache for "white-eyed man," which was how Apaches commonly referred to all whites. Without thinking he took the bowl and swallowed. Searing fire scorched a path down his throat. He thought he would gag. Sputtering, he started to throw the bowl down in anger, then stopped when he realized doing so might make the warrior angry.

"Good," the Apache grunted. He motioned at the bowl. "Drink all. Make you better."

Although Clay would rather have swallowed horse piss, he did as the warrior wanted. Common sense told him that if he was in an Apache wickiup then he must be in an Apache camp somewhere, and depending on where that camp was located, he might be in a heap of trouble. As the old saw went, it appeared that he'd gone from the frying pan into the fire and he didn't have the slightest idea how it had happened.

So girding himself, Clay closed his eyes, held his breath, tilted his head back, and gulped the disgusting brew down before he could get a whiff of the foul odor or fully taste the bitter flavor. It felt as if his innards were being eaten away by acid. His stomach started to heave, and he had to put a hand over his mouth in order not to retch. His whole body shook.

"You do good, white-eye," the warrior said.

Clay gave the bowl to the woman, but never took his eyes off the man. Since the brave was acting so friendly, Clay decided he must be among tame Apaches. He remembered being at the edge of the Dragoon Mountains when the posse strung him up, and since the Dragoons were part of the Chiricahua Reservation, he figured he was in a camp of friendlies somewhere on the southwestern boundary of the reservation. Accordingly, he made bold to speak. "Who are you? How the hell did I get here? I don't savvy any of this."

The warrior showed no emotion whatsoever when he replied, "I am Delgadito."

A tingle of apprehension shot down Clay's spine. Every Arizonan had heard of Delgadito, a bloodthirsty Chiricahua who had left the reservation with a sizeable band and was believed responsible for a number of recent raids on ranches, stage stations, and other points. Delgadito, who had tied several Mexican traders upside down to the spokes of their wagons, then lit fires under their heads. Delgadito, who had massacred the Kline family, new settlers to the region, by impaling every family member on the sharpened tip of a fence post. Suddenly Clay wanted out of there, wanted out of there badly, and he glanced at the door, gauging whether he could reach it before the warrior reached him. There was no way.

"How you called, white man?"

Clay told him.

"Tag-garrrt," Delgadito said, rolling the strange word on the tip of his tongue. Like much of the white tongue, it was alien, hard to say. During the six months he'd tasted reservation life, he'd tried his utmost to master as much English as he could, with disappointing results. He'd hoped to learn more about his enemies by doing so, and thereby discover weaknesses he could exploit, but all he had accomplished was to be able to talk in the tongue as a white child would talk. A small child, at that. He tried the first name instead. "Ka-lay."

Hearing one of the most feared Apache leaders utter his name like a two-year-old was enough to make Clay laugh, had the circumstances been other than what they were. He glanced at the woman, who stood as immobile as a statue, then at Delgadito. For the life of him he couldn't figure out why he was still alive, not when Delgadito hated whites, when Delgadito wanted every last white man laid out as buzzard bait. For that matter, he couldn't figure out how he had survived the hanging. By all rights he should be dead two times over, yet there he sat, battered and sore and hungry as could be, but alive. And he had a good reason to stay alive.

For the first time since reviving, Clay thought of Miles Gillett. Hatred gushed up within him, making his face as red as a beet. His fingers clenched as he thought of wrapping them around Gillett's throat and squeezing.

"We talk later," Delgadito said, turning to go. He stopped when the white man said his name.

"I don't know what you have in mind, but I'd like to talk now, while I'm still able. I want to talk about a trade."

"Trade?" Delgadito repeated, puzzled by the request. Taggart was no trader, of that Delgadito was sure. There was only one thing Delgadito wanted from this man, and he felt confident the man would do it gladly.

"I own a small spread east of Tuscon," Clay explained. "All I have is yours if you'll let me go." It galled him to have to swap for his life, but he would do anything, *anything*, in order to earn his freedom and be able to pay Gillett back. "All my horses, all my cattle, everything. I will turn it over to you free and clear, and I'll never say a word to the law or the Army either."

This was unexpected. Delgadito was a shrewd judge of character, and he had seen enough of his captive to know that here was no coward. Taggart wasn't begging for his life. There was no fear in the big man's voice. Something else, though. Delgadito looked into Taggart's eyes and recognized the rage simmering in their depths, but not rage directed at him, rage directed elsewhere, the same sort of rage he had seen at the hanging. Delgadito had never known any man filled with so much constant burning anger. Even Fiero had his calm moments.

"I know what you're thinking," Clay said. "You figure I'm lying, that I'm trying to trick you to save my hide." He paused. "I won't have any use for anything anyway after I do what I have to do, so what difference does it make if I let you have what you want? And no matter what else I may be, I'm no liar. My word is my bond."

"Bond?" Delgadito said.

"I speak with a straight tongue," Clay clarified.

"Yes. I see that, white man. But I not want ranch, not want cattle."

"Then what? Money? I don't have much, but what I have is yours."

"Of what use money to us?"

"Rifles then? Or pistols?" Clay said, and hesitated. He had always thought that anyone who dealt guns to Indians deserved to be staked out alive on an ant hill, but this was a special circumstance. Unless he persuaded the renegade to accept his offer, he'd never have his revenge on Gillett. "I can get you those if you want."

"Another time, yes," Delgadito said rather sadly.

"You mean in a few days? A week? Or what do you call it?" Clay pondered a moment. "In a moon? How long?"

"Not long. Never."

"I don't savvy."

"Can you walk?"

"Walk where?" Clay asked suspiciously. He didn't trust the redskin for a minute, and he had heard enough of the devious Apache mind to suspect treachery at every turn.

"Come," Delgadito said, gesturing at the entrance. His dealings with whites had taught him how they thought, and he knew that in order to have this white-eye do as he wanted, he must show why he wanted it done. Otherwise Ka-lay would balk.

Clay didn't see where he had any choice but to do as he was bid. Putting both hands flat on the ground, he pushed up, and was surprised to find he was stronger than he expected to be. He noticed another bowl lying near where his head had been on the blanket, a bowl containing dried traces of the same concoction the woman had fed him, and he deduced that she had given him more while he was unconscious. Whatever the horrible brew might be, it had done wonders for his constitution. He felt strong enough to wrestle a bear. But he advanced slowly, keeping one eye on the warrior's knife.

Delgadito saw and his own eyes lit with secret delight. Here was a white man worthy of respect, he reflected, a man smart enough not to trust an enemy no matter how friendly the enemy might appear. Delgadito stood aside so Ka-lay could go out first.

Clay blinked in the bright afternoon sunlight. He discovered he was in a spacious hollow in which many other wickiups had been erected, and he saw dozens of Apaches going about their daily tasks. Over by a spring were several women who stared at him and tittered. Husky warriors gazed at him as if sizing him up for a scalping.

Delgadito heard the laughter, saw that his captive appeared to be upset, and surmising the women were to blame, silenced them with a single glance.

"How long was I out?" Clay asked.

Pointing at the sun, Delgadito made a sweeping motion from horizon to horizon.

"One day?"

"We talk," Delgadito said, anxious to get to the issue of most importance. "I . . ." he went on, and stopped, trying to find the right word. The many talks he had shared with the agent came to mind, and from one of them he plucked the word he hoped was right. "Explain now."

"Explain what?"

"Why we take you. Why we *save* white man,"
Delgadito said. "If not for us, you die." He deliberately stressed the fact that they had come to the
man's rescue to arouse the man's gratitude, and in
this he seemed to succeed.

"I'm glad you did what you did," Clay said,
"although for the life of me I can't figure out
why."

"For peace."

"What peace?"

"Our peace," Delgadito said, encompassing the
camp with the sweep of an arm.

"Are you telling me that *you* want to sue for peace
with the government?" Clay asked incredulously,
adding without thinking, "After all you've done, you
have your nerve." He involuntarily tensed, expecting
the Apache to be mad, but there was no reaction
whatsoever.

"You see why," Delgadito said. "Look."

"Look where?"

"Look," Delgadito persisted, nodding at several
others.

Confused, Clay scanned the encampment. All he
saw was a typical Apache camp, exactly like those
he had occasionally passed when he'd delivered his
cattle to the reservation. There were the same dome-
shaped wickiups, the same darkly sinister men, the
same overworked women, and the same grimy children. There was nothing out of the ordinary. "I don't
see . . ." he began.

"Look harder."

Annoyed, Clay slowly turned, studying everything.
He was halfway around when it hit him, and when it
did, he recoiled as if struck. This camp was not, in
fact, like any of the others. There were differences
apparent even to someone like him who knew little
of Apache life.

For one thing, the wickiups were more crudely built than Clay remembered. Either from a lack of the proper materials, or haste in building, there were gaps in the sides where the wind and rain could get through, and some of the dwellings were made of branches and grass so dry that a stray spark from a fire would set them fully ablaze in an instant.

For another thing, Clay noticed the clothing worn by these Apaches was in bad need of repair. Shirts, leggings, dresses, moccasins, all were torn or worn through in spots and far dirtier than he recalled Apache clothes being. The Apaches themselves were dirtier, some downright filthy, as if they rarely took the time to clean themselves.

Finally, Clay realized that here were the leanest Apaches he had ever beheld. The men were still stocky by white standards, but they had less meat on them than warriors on the reservation. The same with the women and the children, who appeared even worse off. A few of the former were little more than skin and bones, and many of the latter, who went around bare-chested, were so thin their ribs showed through their skin.

"What the hell?" Clay said.

"Now you savvy?" Delgadito asked.

"Your people are starving."

"My people hungry, yes. Never plenty food. Never plenty game." Delgadito extended an arm toward five gaunt horses. "Last ones. Eat one each day. When they gone, we much hungrier."

Clay saw a chance to make his case again. "All the more reason for you to take me up on my offer. My cattle would feed your band for many months."

"Where we hide many cattle?" Delgadito responded. "Army come. Soldiers track us, find us, kill us. No." He watched a small girl who was sucking on a shriveled piece of root. "Need peace. Want live on reservation."

"The government should be right pleased when you tell them."

Delgadito turned. "You tell them."

"Me?" Clay said.

"Army believe you. Say Delgadito save. Say Delgadito good friend. Army not punish Delgadito's people."

At last Clay understood, and the cleverness of the Apache's scheme made him throw back his head and laugh. The wily bastard had spared him from hanging so he could speak on the band's behalf! Given the Army's treatment of renegades, Delgadito would be shot on sight if he dared to show his face anywhere on the reservation. The same held true for the other warriors. Delgadito needed a go-between and he had picked Clay.

"Why you laugh, white-eye?"

"You're an *hombre* after my own heart," Clay declared, relief coursing through him as he realized he wasn't going to be slain after all. If playing along with the Apaches would earn him the chance at the vengeance he craved, then by God he'd do whatever they asked and make no bones about doing it.

Delgadito did not quite comprehend the white man's statement, but the friendly tone was obvious. "You talk to Army? You help us?"

"Sure I will," Clay said, so pleased at the state of affairs he beamed like an idiot until a troubling thought occurred to him. Thanks to Gillett, in the eyes of the law he had been a wanted man. That was why he had fled with the posse on his heels. If word had gotten to the Army, they'd slap irons on him the minute he showed up and hold him for Marshal Crane. He'd be worse off then ever, because the next time Crane would do the hanging right.

"Is something wrong?" Delgadito asked on noticing a cloud that seemed to come over the white man's features.

"No. Not a thing," Clay lied. Telling the truth might get him killed. Once the Apaches found he couldn't be of any use to them, they'd have no cause to keep him alive.

"Good." Delgadito surveyed the camp, barely able to hide his feelings at the destitute state of his people. All the running, all the fighting, had gotten them nowhere, had accomplished nothing. Their clothes were little better than rags, their bellies often cried for nourishment, and they couldn't enjoy a moment's peace, not when the Army's Indian trackers might find them at any moment.

Fleeing the Chiricahua Reservation had seemed like the right thing to do at the time, yet now Delgadito deeply regretted ever having persuaded his band to do it. With the Army nipping at their heels, they had made for Mexico, the warriors fighting a delaying action every foot of the way so the women and children could reach Mexico safely.

Delgadito had thought they would be safe south of the border. He knew that U.S. troops were rarely allowed to cross the strange, invisible line the whites recognized as their boundary. And he also knew how inexperienced and ineffective the Mexican troops were. He'd figured on reaching a remote haven in the mountains and living there undisturbed, but he had not counted on the scalp hunters.

South of the border were two Mexican states which the Apaches had always roamed at will. One of those states, Chihuahua, was on friendly terms with Delgadito's people. But the other, Sonora, had openly declared war on all Indians, and had gone so far as to pay a bounty for Indian scalps, whether man, woman, or child.

As a result, vicious bands of scalp hunters now roved Sonora hunting for victims. And these killers were not very particular about who they ambushed. Delgadito had heard stories to the effect that many peaceful Indians were being secretly set upon and butchered and their hair turned over to the authorities for the blood money.

Delgadito's flight into Mexico had been cut off by just such a cutthroat bunch. Fiero and others had wanted to fight the scalp hunters, but Delgadito, concerned for their families, had convinced them to retreat toward the Dragoons. He'd simply not been sure his followers would survive a clash. The men who made their living taking scalps were undeniably fierce and almost as adept at living off the land as Indians themselves. Many were half-breeds who hated the Indian half of their ancestry. They were cruel men who would not hesitate to slay the tiniest infant, and Delgadito had not cared to tempt fate by clashing with them.

So now here Delgadito stood, his dream of a safe haven shattered, his hope for the future of his people gone. He had stooped so low as to rely on the aid of a white man so a meeting could be set up with the Army. He was weary of running, weary of fighting, a shell of his former self, and he knew it.

Just then Cuchillo Negro came over.

Clay had been watching the women at the spring. He turned toward Delgadito, and was surprised on finding another warrior had joined them. There had been no sound, not the faintest scraping of a leather sole, no warning at all. It was as if the warrior had sprung from the very air.

"Fiero and El Chico have still not come back," Cuchillo Negro reported. "You said you wanted to know."

"Where could they be?" Delgadito said. "There is no better horse thief than Fiero. No matter how many he stole, he should have been back by now."

"Do you want someone to go look for them?"

"Ask Pasqual. He reads sign better than any of us."

A horse whinnied as Cuchillo Negro started to run off, and both men paused to glance at the five animals. Two of the horses had their heads up, their ears pricked, and were gazing westward. Delgadito looked at the rim of the hollow, where Azul was keeping watch. "Is all well?" he called out.

"Yes," Azul answered, his tone betraying his boredom.

Delgadito faced the white man. "In three sleeps we go reservation. You come with us."

"Whatever you want," Clay answered. In truth, he had no choice, and he would have to make the best of the situation and hope the Army wouldn't throw him in the guardhouse.

The same horse whinnied again.

Pivoting, Delgadito stared at the animal, mentally vowing to add it to the cooking pot that very evening if it didn't stop alarming them for no reason. The culprit, a bay reduced to skin and bones from hunger, was again staring westward. On an impulse Delgadito climbed to the rim and stared out over the arid countryside. To the west was the mouth of a dry wash, barren but for a few cactus and weeds. To the north were brown hills, as lifeless as the desert to the south. Not a creature stirred anywhere. He saw no cause to be concerned.

Azul walked up. "Is something wrong?"

"We eat the bay tonight," Delgadito said. He began to retrace his steps, but he hadn't taken more than two strides down the slope when the hot air was shattered by a single gunshot, coming from the west. Wet drops splattered on Delgadito's neck. He whirled, his hand dropping to his knife, just as Azul, arms outspread, forehead blown outward by a heavy caliber slug, toppled over on top of him. Delgadito tried to get his arms up but the dead weight and momentum bowled him over, while from all sides there arose a savage chorus of whoops, yells, and gunfire.

The camp was under attack.

Chapter Four

Clay Taggart was standing right where Delgadito had
left him, right out in the open where he was exposed
for all to see. He became painfully aware of this with
the very first volley as slugs bit into the earth all
around him and a bullet nicked his left thigh. The
stinging pain overcame his initial shock, and he was
already in motion, diving behind a nearby wickiup,
when a second ragged volley tore into the stunned
Apaches.

Men appeared all along the rim of the hollow,
somber, deadly men, whites and Mexicans and
breeds all armed with the latest Winchesters and
pistols. They made no threats, gave no warning, but
simply cut loose with cold, methodical precision.

Clay, flat on the ground, heard the drumming of
hoofs. Peering past the wickiup, he saw horsemen
pouring into the mouth of the basin, firing as
they charged, some with swords or Bowie knives
in hand which they wielded with savage glee. The

Apaches were coming to life, the warriors fighting back while the women gathered their children and tried to flee.

Clay had no idea what was going on. The hard-cases swarming into the encampment weren't regular Army troops, nor did they have the look of typical townsmen. No, these were hardened killers, each and every one.

A warrior put an arrow into one of the attackers, and was riddled with gunfire in return. A woman trying to usher a little girl to safety was shot through the head. The little girl, moments later, was trampled under the flailing hoofs of a horse. Three other children were blasted to pieces. Another woman, scrambling desperately up the east incline, had her head cleaved clear down to the chin by a glittering sword.

The slaughter was awful, indescribable. For every one of the attacking band who was wounded or slain, four or five Apaches fell. Clay had never seen the like. He was rooted in place, transfixed by the carnage. Or at least he was until suddenly a rider appeared in front of the wickiup, spotted him, and smirking, started to lift a rifle.

"I'm a white man!" Clay bellowed, thinking the news would see him spared. But to his consternation, the rider kept lifting the rifle. Clay knew he would be shot if he didn't do something, so he did the only thing he could think of. Surging to his feet, he flung two handfuls of dirt into the mount's face.

Neighing, the horse pranced backward, bobbing its head as it did. The man in the saddle had to lower his rifle and tighten his hold on the reins to keep control.

Which bought Clay the precious seconds he needed to whirl and flee around the back of the wickiup. A bullet whizzed by. Close at hand a woman screamed. Children were wailing, men shouting oaths in several tongues. Constant war whoops rent the hot air. The scene was one of utter bedlam.

Clay flew past a bush, glanced up at the rim, and spied a Mexican in a sombrero taking aim at him. Darting to the left just as the rifle cracked, he ducked behind a prickly pear. The rifleman shifted, sighting on an Apache, so Clay rose and ran farther south, seeking a way out. He saw a warrior on the slope, saw another dead nearby. As the warrior sprang like a cornered panther at a horseman, he recognized Delgadito.

The grizzled rider never knew what struck him. The man had his back to the incline, and was shooting into a group of fleeing women when Delgadito landed astride the horse behind the saddle, seized him by the hair, and slit his throat with a neat, swift stroke. Without waiting for the lifeblood to spurt out, Delgadito shoved the rider off, slid forward into the saddle, and galloped at another enemy.

Clay watched in awe as Delgadito rode straight into a second horseman, the collision bowling over both animals and pinning the attacker under his. Delgadito leaped clear at the last moment, pounced on his struggling foe, and dispatched the man with a thrust to the heart.

Other hand-to-hand clashes had broken out all along the basin. The warriors were outnumbered, their situation almost hopeless, yet they fought on with a ferocity the attackers could scarcely hope to match. There was a fanatical desperation to the Apaches' stand, a desperation sparked by the dangers their women and children faced. They were literal red devils, and for a short while it appeared they were holding their own.

Clay knew better. He realized the outcome was a foregone conclusion. And he had to get out of there before the warriors were wiped out. Once the hardcases finished with the men, they'd turn their full attention on however many women and children were left—not to mention him, provided he was still alive.

The shape of the hollow favored the attacking force. Narrow at the opening and wider back near the spring, it formed a natural bottleneck. Apparently the Apaches had chosen the site because it offered a perfect hiding place for such a large group, counting on their constant vigilance to warn them of approaching enemies in time to escape if need be. But for once they had been caught napping.

The slopes were steep, but not so steep a man couldn't walk up them. Running up was another matter, since the loose dirt made for slippery footing. Vegetation was sparse, although along the west side a row of mostly dry brush offered slight cover.

Crouching, Clay studied the rim, noting how far apart the attackers were spaced. There weren't as many as he had at first thought, although more than enough to keep the Apaches pinned in the hollow. Most were closer to the wickiups than the opening of the hollow, and Clay noticed a 30-foot stretch of rim near the opening that was clear of gunmen. Directly below that stretch was the dry brush.

Clay headed toward that point. He covered a half-dozen feet and checked behind him, wary of being run down. Not far off was Delgadito, locked in mortal combat with a hefty half-breed. The two separated. The breed aimed a revolver and fired at point-blank range, but for some reason the pistol misfired and the next moment Delgadito buried his knife in the breed's chest. Yanking the bloody blade out, Delgadito turned, looking for another enemy to fight. Up on the east rim a rifle thundered and the Apache crumpled, tottering rearward until he tripped over a stone.

Forever after, Clay Taggart could never explain to his own or anyone else's satisfaction exactly what made him go to the Apache's aid. He should have kept on going, should have saved his own hide. If he had, Arizona would never have known that terrible period in its early history known as the Reign of the White Apache.

Maybe it was the fact that Delgadito had spared Clay's life. Maybe it was that Delgadito's woman had been nursing Clay back to health. Or maybe Clay actually felt some sort of fledgling friendship for the Scourge of the Southwest. Whatever the reason, instead of fleeing, Clay spun and raced to where Delgadito lay. A red stream gushed from a nasty gash in the warrior's temple, but the Apache still breathed. Kneeling, Clay got both brawny arms under Delgadito, strained, and stood, his knees nearly buckling in the process.

Clay trotted to the southwest. He would have died then and there since he was such an easy target burdened as he was, but by a sheer whim of Fate the remaining Apaches chose that moment to launch a counterattack on the riflemen lining the west rim. The horsemen and the killers on the east rim, seeing their friends in danger, forgot about everyone else and poured their fire into the charging warriors.

Clay was halfway to the brush when, on stepping on a sharp spine of jagged rock, he was reminded that he wasn't wearing any boots or shoes. In all the excitement he had completely forgotten. Wincing, he shut the torment from his mind and pressed on, his soles scorched by the burning soil. Miraculously he reached the brush. There were no gaps, no way through that he could see, so firming his grip on

Delgadito, Clay barreled through to the other side. Tiny branches seared into his flesh. His feet felt as if they were cut to shreds by razors.

Then Clay was facing the barren slope and the daunting task of climbing to the rim while burdened by the Apache. He hurried upward, digging in his heels with each step, the muscles in his legs and thighs bulging. Several times he slipped, and once he smacked onto a knee, causing him to clamp his teeth onto his lip to keep from crying out.

Partway up, Clay heard a piercing shriek of abject terror and looked back. One of the attacking force, a huge man with a brown beard who wore an old Union cap, had seized a small child and was sinking his sword into the youngster again and again while the child's mother beat futilely at him. The man flung the child down with contempt, spun, and nearly decapitated the mother.

Thankfully the rim had buckled at that spot, forming a gap through which Clay plunged. He didn't look before he leaped, and as a result he found himself tumbling head over heels down an even steeper incline. In a swirl of dust he came to rest, Delgadito at his side.

The warrior groaned as Clay lifted him again. Since the riflemen were to the north and east, and to the south the desert shimmered in the sun, Clay could only go west. He ran as best he was able, avoiding rocks and cactus that would tear his feet apart. In the hollow the firing, whooping, and yelling reached a crescendo.

Clay made for the mouth of a dry wash, glancing repeatedly over his shoulder. He half expected to feel a slug tear through his back at any time, but the riflemen on the rim were too busy shooting Apaches to bother looking behind them. One time when he glanced back, he blundered into a small cactus and clamped his teeth tight so he wouldn't yelp in pain. Tiny barbs jutted from his big toe when he gained the wash and hastened around a bend.

Once screened from the attackers, Clay sank down and let Delgadito roll free. He plucked gingerly at the barbs and thought of the man in the Union Army cap. For some reason he felt he should know that man. Not personally, for he was sure they had never met. He figured he must have heard of the man somewhere. Then, as the last barb came out, taking a small piece of his flesh with it, Clay remembered.

Ben Johnson was one of the most notorious scalp hunters south of the border. A Union deserter, he had drifted to Tuscon after the war, made himself unpopular with practically everyone, and fled into Mexico a few years ago after killing an unarmed prospector in a saloon. The last word Clay had heard was to the effect that Johnson was the leader of a band working for the Sonoran government, tracking down Apaches and lifting their hair for a hefty bounty.

No one had told Clay that Johnson was now operating north of the border as well. Maybe, Clay mused, this was the first time. It had just been Clay's dumb luck to be in the wrong place at the wrong time, and he was damned fortunate to be alive. But for how long? Once the scalp hunters were done massacring the Apaches, they might fan out and search the countryside. Clay had to keep moving.

Delgadito was as limp as a wet rag. Clay had a hard time getting the warrior off the ground, and once in motion his hips and legs protested the burden. He firmed his grip, then forged on, counting every step he took as being one step closer to saving his hide, to getting clean away. The sun was scorching hot on his back, so hot he sweated profusely. His feet ached, as did his spine, yet he refused to stop.

Clay lost all track of time. He had to keep going no matter what, so keep going he did, even when his body began to give out, when fatigue made each stride an effort in itself. He settled into a rhythm, moving first one leg, then the other, focusing on nothing else but his legs, plodding on long after most other men would have given up.

It was the unbearable heat that brought Clay down. After hours of walking, his limbs were leaden, his vision blurred, and his feet hurting so fiercely the pain in itself was mildly numbing. His mouth was terribly dry, his lips beginning to crack. Inside his chest an inferno raged, making breathing hard to do. He inhaled, but all that poured into his lungs was more fire. So sick he could hardly hold Delgadito, he stumbled, tried to right himself, tripped, and fell.

Clay saw the ground rushing up to meet his face. He wanted to cushion the fall with his palms, but after all he had been through he was too weak to lift his arms. The last thing he remembered was his temple seeming to split apart and his lungs turning to flames.

A cool breeze fanning Delgadito's face brought the warrior back to the land of the living. He sat up, looked all around in confusion, and tried to stand. Searing pangs in his head made him double over instead. His fingers found the cause, a deep gash on his temple gouged out by a bullet. A fraction deeper and he would have died.

Delgadito steeled himself against the torment. From early childhood the boys of his tribe were taught how to bear up under great pain without complaint. Their lives and the lives of their fellows often depended on their stoicism, since a single outcry might be all that was needed to bring a hostile force down on them.

Now Delgadito got to his knees. Rare weakness
caused him to prop himself up with his hands. Overhead, stars sparkled. From the northwest wafted the
breeze that had revived him. In the east hung a full
moon. Glancing to his left, he was shocked to see
the white man lying nearby. He looked around and
realized they were miles from the camp, in rugged country where he had often hunted antelope.
How had they gotten there? Delgadito wondered.
He remembered nothing after being shot.

The only logical explanation was that others had
carried them from the hollow, but when Delgadito
was finally able to stand he saw no one else anywhere. It was just the white man and him. He bent
over, placing a hand next to the white-eye's lips.
Shallow breaths showed the man was still alive.

Straightening, Delgadito walked in a small circle,
still convinced some of his people must have saved
him. He checked the ground, his eagle eyes easily
reading the impressions in the dirt. To his surprise he found only one set of tracks, those of
the white-eye, tracks deeper than they should be,
so deep that obviously the man had been carrying
something heavy. Or someone.

Delgadito knelt by Clay Taggart. He knew now
who had saved him, and that the white man had
about used himself up in doing so. Mystified,
Delgadito stared at the pale features of the only
white he had ever shown any degree of mercy to,
and then only because he had needed to use the man
for his own purposes. Why, he asked himself, had the
white man done what he had done? They were mortal enemies. The white-eye should have left Delgadito
to be scalped and butchered, not saved him.

For the longest while Delgadito stayed where he
was, staring. Then he rose, searched about for a flat
stone of suitable size with a smooth edge, and went

off into the night in search of a certain cactus. He had to range far afield before he spotted the familiar barrel shape. Kneeling beside the plant, he carefully chipped away with the stone, being careful not to prick himself on the spines. A knife would have made the job much easier, but his was gone.

Eventually Delgadito had chopped off a sizeable chunk, including a generous portion of pulp. Rising, he retraced his steps to where he had left the white man. Those less skilled would have been hopelessly lost, unable to tell north from south, but Delgadito relied on the positions of the stars and his extraordinary memory of the terrain to bring him to the exact spot.

Clay Taggart lay on his side, still breathing shallowly. Delgadito crouched and rolled the man over, then roughly gave Taggart's chin a shake. When there was no reaction, he shook again.

To Clay, it felt as if his mouth was in the grip of a vise. Vaguely he became aware of wind on his body and anguish in his feet. He opened his eyes, saw in the gloom the swarthy face of an Apache looming above him, and started to scramble up in alarm. A voice he knew stopped him.

"Suck, Ka-lay."

"What?" Clay blurted out, and wished he hadn't as his mouth flared with pain.

"Suck," Delgadito repeated, raising the chunk of barrel cactus to the white man's mouth.

Clay began to recoil, then thought better of the notion. The warrior was trying to help him. So he parted his lips and tasted the thin, watery sap of a cactus for the very first time. He wanted to tear into the moist pulp and gulp it down, but the Apache had told him to suck, so suck was all he did. There wasn't much to drink, but what little he swallowed was the most refreshing liquid Clay had ever quenched a thirst with. When he was done he asked, "Where's yours?"

"I drink later," Delgadito said, tossing the cactus aside. "Come. We go now."

"Where to?" Clay asked as the warrior grasped him by the elbow and hoisted him to his feet. His soles hurt so much he nearly collapsed; he felt as if he was walking on bits of broken glass.

"My people." Turning, Delgadito took a step, but he had to halt when Clay grabbed his arm.

"Hold on there, pardner. We can't go running off in the middle of the night like this. We ought to wait until first light, when we can see what the hell we're doing."

"I see well," Delgadito said. Again he started to depart, again the white man stopped him.

"You're not listening," Clay said. "You didn't see what I saw after you were hit. If any of your people are still alive, it's a miracle."

"Miracle?"

"The hand of God," Clay explained. When the warrior showed no sign of comprehending, he clarified by adding, "The will of the Great Spirit or whatever you call it."

"We go," Delgadito said, jerking his arm loose. The reference to spirits made no sense to him. The whites were ignorant in that regard, and knew nothing of the *Gans*. Once he had discussed such matters with the agent on the reservation, and had been dumbfounded to learn the white God taught that all people should love one another and always turn the other cheek when set upon. The idea had been so ridiculous as to be unbelievable, just another example of the strange ways of the Americans.

As every one of Delgadito's tribe knew, there were only two virtues that truly counted: stealing without being caught and killing without being killed. In a world filled with enemies, those were the traits that insured survival. All else was of secondary importance.

So now, on hearing Ka-lay talk so foolishly, Delgadito kept on going. He felt no deep obligation to the white man. If the rancher came, fine. If not, that was fine with Delgadito too. He knew the white-eye had saved him, but the act did not bind him to Delgadito as a brother. In Delgadito's eyes they were still enemies, existing under a temporary truce. Delgadito had not brought the cactus as an act of kindness. Rather, Delgadito had wanted the man to be strong enough to make the return journey and he knew how refreshing the pulp could be.

Clay stared at the warrior's broad back, debating whether to go along. He was of half a mind to tell the Apache to go to hell, but then he gazed out over the moonlit landscape and realized he didn't have more than a hazy idea where he was or how to reach the nearest settlement. When the sun rose he might be able to tell, but how long would he last on his own?

Clay wavered until he glanced down at the discarded cactus. Delgadito had done him a kindness in bringing it, had gone to extra effort to revive Clay and provide some nourishment. The least Clay could do was give the brave the benefit of the doubt and offer his own hand in possible friendship. "Wait," he called, hurrying forward.

Delgadito set a brisk pace. His head throbbed and the rib he had cracked in the collision of the two horses ached abominably, but he wasn't about to quit shy of his destination. After a while he noticed the white-eye was limping, and was annoyed to find the man could not keep up. He would have left then and there, but he had another use for Ka-lay and did not want to lose him. So Delgadito slowed without being obvious about doing so, and they hiked on in silence.

Clay was thinking of ways to reach civilization. He needed a new horse, new clothes, new weapons. Most of all he had to get his hands on some money, without which he couldn't buy any of the things he needed. There was a poke filled with coins hidden on his spread, his stash for when times were lean, but reaching it posed an insurmountable problem.

The farther Clay walked, the more his feet bothered him. He knew his soles hung in tattered strips, knew there were blisters galore from his heels to his toes, but he didn't bother to examine them closely. It was best if he didn't know; sometimes pain was better tolerated if a man didn't realize how badly off he really was.

Thankfully, the cool night air helped Clay keep his strength up, invigorating him after the scalding heat of the day. He still craved water, but not as desperately as before. After the first mile he flagged, but he was proud of being able to keep up with the Apache, and flattered himself that he was recovering faster than he would have dreamed he could.

It seemed as if an eternity went by. Clay was flagging even more, and he noticed Delgadito did not appear very pleased. He thought the Apache might up and desert him, and he redoubled his efforts. When, shortly thereafter, the warrior suddenly stopped, spun, and placed a hand on Clay's chest, Clay was sure they would be going their separate ways. Then Clay heard gruff laughter, and peering ahead he saw flickering light dancing along the rim of the hollow, which wasn't more than 20 feet off. He also saw a sentry moving along the rim in their direction.

Chapter Five

Clay Taggart's first reaction was to turn and run
before he was shot dead where he stood, but he had
no more than started to whirl when hands as hard
as solid stone clamped onto his shoulders and he
was yanked to the earth so swiftly his teeth snapped
together. Delgadito was at his side, as motionless
as a log. Clay imitated the Apache. A tremendous
itching broke out between his shoulder blades, and
it was all he could do not to reach over his shoulder
to scratch.

Whistling softly, the sentry drew even with their
position. Abruptly, he paused to stare out over the
foreboding terrain.

Clay saw, and he was astounded the man didn't
spot them. Then he remembered the sentry had
been staring toward the fire moments ago and
would not be able to see much of anything until
his eyes adjusted. Once that happened, the man was
certain to notice the odd figures below. Clay wished

he had a six-shooter, a rifle, anything he could use to defend himself.

The sentry coughed, ran a hand through his beard, and strolled on, still whistling.

Delgadito shifted, placing his mouth close to Clay's ear. "Keep watch," he whispered.

"What . . ." Clay began, then fell silent as the warrior darted up the incline so rapidly Clay would have missed the movement had he blinked. He saw the Apache slip over the rim and tensed for an outburst of yells and gunshots, but there was none. Clay was alone with the night.

Inside the basin, Delgadito went down the slope like a scuttling lizard and slid to a stop behind a bush. From there he could see charred remains of wickiups, a huge campfire, and the rowdy men around it. Many were drinking and laughing. They had won a great victory and were celebrating.

Delgadito checked the rim. There were two other sentries, none close to his position. Snaking forward, he went to the next cover, a rock the size of his head. From there to a rut in the ground, and from there to another bush. Bit by bit he worked across the hollow, his dark eyes on the spot where his wickiup had stood.

About 30 yards from his goal Delgadito rounded a bush and stopped on inhaling the pungent odor of death: blood and gore mixed in a drying puddle. Beside the puddle lay a woman, a new hole between her eyes, her scalp completely gone. For once Delgadito's training failed him. He trembled and hissed like an enraged sidewinder, and had not the breach of self-discipline jarred him into regaining his self-control, he might have risen and mindlessly hurled himself at the nearby scalp hunters.

Going on proved a nightmare. Every few feet Delgadito found another body. Warriors, women, and children had been ruthlessly slaughtered, and every last one, including the youngest of little ones, had lost his hair to the razor knives of the greedy killers. Delgadito had known them all, known them all well. Many were relatives, many good friends.

Then, when within a dozen feet of his former wickiup, Delgadito found those he sought: his woman, his *ish-tia-nay*, and their two children. Her body lay on top of the two boys, showing she had been trying to shield them when all three were shot again and again. There were too many bullet holes to count. Someone had taken sadistic glee in their deaths.

Delgadito lay still, burning the sight into his memory, every wound, every bloody splotch, every smudge of dirt. He wanted to always remember so that he would never again be as weak as he had been when he'd decided to return to the reservation and meekly live as the Americans dictated. Whites had done this, whites and Mexicans and breeds, but it was the white-eyes he hated most simply because they were the ones who had broken the spirit of his people and taken the land that his forefathers had roamed at will for more generations than any man could count.

There was another aspect to Delgadito's weakness, an aspect that made his saliva bitter to the taste. He had done it for *them*, had fled from the scalp hunters to protect the lives of those in his band, especially the lives of the women and children. And what had running gotten him? Gotten them? He was a leader without anyone to lead, a husband without a wife, a father without children. In a sense, he was now a Shis-Inday without a tribe.

Delgadito reached out, touching his fingertips to those of his woman. In his mind he said to her, "I will avenge your death. Although I fight on alone, I will never let them break my spirit. I will make them pay in blood for the blood they have shed. And when I am done, I will join you on the other side." Then, turning, he began to retrace his route.

Outside the hollow, Clay Taggart waited nervously for the warrior to show. Taggart wasn't a worrier by nature, but the harrowing events of the past few days had stripped him of his usual self-confidence, not to mention his guns and his clothes. He wanted to get the hell out of there before they were discovered. He wanted to live long enough to strangle the life from Miles Gillett.

Suddenly Clay saw the same sentry returning. Each sentry had a certain area to cover, walking endlessly back and forth. The fact the scalp hunters had seen fit to post guards told Clay that some of the Apaches must have escaped. He huddled down low, flush with the ground, and mentally cursed Delgadito for putting his life in peril. Had he known what Delgadito was doing at that very moment, he would have cursed aloud, guard or no guard.

For the object of the rancher's anger had frozen on hearing the clomp of footsteps, seen a drunken half-breed weaving toward some brush, and angled to intercept the man. A revolver was on the breed's right hip, a Bowie knife on his left. And Delgadito needed weapons.

The scalp hunter walked behind the brush, giggling to himself as he thought of the day's slaughter and the bag of coins he would earn for his part in the massacre. He hitched at his britches, then felt his knife sheath move slightly. Raising his left hand, he was surprised to find the knife was gone, and he assumed it had somehow slipped out. Then fingers touched his privates, but they weren't his fingers, and a sharp pain speared through his groin. Dumbly, he looked down. Dumbly, he realized what had happened and opened his mouth to scream. Another pain, this time in his chest, cut off his scream, and the last sight he saw as he sank down was the stony face of an Apache.

Delgadito wasted no time in removing the breed's gun belt, to which the sheath was attached, and belting it around his waist. Having fought breeds before, he knew to bend over and run a hand inside each of the man's boots. He was rewarded with another knife, a glittering dagger. A check of the man's pockets turned up a watch, which Delgadito cast aside; coins, which he dropped into the half-breed's open mouth; and a derringer, which he kept for himself.

Like a specter Delgadito flitted across the hollow, moving swiftly now in case the dead man should be soon missed. He was nearly to the wall when a shout confirmed it. But the shout drew the attention of all the sentries to the men at the fire, and while they were blinded by the light, Delgadito slipped out into the night. He moved soundlessly to where he had left the rancher, coming up on Ka-lay from the rear.

Now Delgadito paused. Here was a white-eye and he had vowed to kill them all. His hand strayed to the Bowie and he started to ease the blade out. A quick stab and he would be on his own. He would have done the deed too, had not a picture of Ka-lay carrying him for miles on blistered feet caused him to hesitate. More weakness, he told himself, and drew the knife a fraction higher. Then he recalled the new use he wanted to make of the man, and he let go of the hilt. Not now, he thought. I will wait for the right time.

When Clay felt a hand touch his leg he jumped, and might have yelped too had not a hand covered his mouth. If someone once told him that one day he would be exceedingly glad to hear the voice of an Apache renegade, he would have laughed the person to scorn. Yet glad he was, although he muttered, "About damn time."

"Come," Delgadito said, and was off, bearing to the north, then to the northeast, going around the hollow and into the hills that would take them to the Dragoon Mountains.

The brief rest had restored some of Clay's vitality. For a mile he ran fairly well. Then gradually the aching in his feet worsened. At two miles he was limping again, and he was unsure how long he would last.

Delgadito stopped and regarded the white man without expression. Inwardly, he marveled for perhaps the hundredth time that the Americans had been able to defeat his people when Americans were so weak. Individually, that is. Their great strength lay in their numbers, which were as numerous as the shifting grains of sand in the desert to the south. That, and their guns, their very superior guns which could fire six times or more without reloading, and the huge guns the Army used, guns capable of spitting death from a great distance and blowing apart whole mountains. Those were the reasons his people were now virtual slaves. Had the contest been even, had it been man-to-man, the Shis-Inday would still be roaming wild and free.

Delgadito liked to think of the struggle between the two peoples as a struggle between a bear and ants. His people had always revered the bear, had shunned eating the meat of the wise one, so comparing them to the bear was natural. As everyone knew, any single bear could kill any single ant with ease. But when there were ants without end, ants whose stings could hurt even the mighty bear, what chance did the bear have? In the long run, the bear, like the Shis-Inday, would succumb. And here Delgadito was, sparing the life of one of these ants!

"Sit," Delgadito said. Squatting, he examined the man's feet in the moonlight. They were terribly mangled. Unless he did something, the rancher would collapse before dawn. "This help," he declared, hastily removing his shirt.

Clay didn't know quite what to think. Apaches weren't famous for their acts of charity, yet he couldn't deny the evidence of his own eyes. The warrior was cutting off the shirt sleeves. He made no comment as Delgadito slipped first one sleeve, then the other, over his feet and tied them at both ends so they would stay on. It wasn't much protection, but it would have to do.

"Better some, Ka-lay?"

"It's Clay. One word." Clay pronounced his name again, exaggerating it so the warrior would understand. In doing so he inadvertently gave the word two syllables and didn't realize he was doing so.

Delgadito did not see any difference. To his ears he was saying it properly. He was annoyed to be reminded of his difficulty in mastering the white tongue, so he said, "I give you new name. Lickoyee-shis-inday." He did so in sarcasm, to make light of the white man's weakness.

"Thanks," Clay said, sincerely flattered since he believed the act was one of genuine friendship. "What does it mean?"

"White Shis-Inday."

"What does Shis-Inday mean?"

Delgadito tapped a thick thumb on his chest. "Shis-Inday."

"But I thought your handle was Delgadito?"

"Handle?"

"Your name. Or at least how you like to be called. I've heard that you Apaches use Spanish names so no one will know your real names. It's bad medicine or something like that."

"My name Delgadito. I am Shis-Inday."

Clay still didn't understand. "You're an Apache."

"Others call my people Apache. We call Shis-Inday."

"But I've heard Apaches call themselves Apaches," Clay mentioned.

"Among others, yes. When alone, not so all time."

"I think I savvy," Clay said. "Shis-Inday is the name your people have always called themselves. Apache is what everyone else always calls you, so you use it sometimes yourselves. Where did the word Apache come from?"

"Not know."

"What does Shis-Inday mean in English?" Clay asked, not so much out of any real interest in knowing so much as to gain a little more rest time.

Answering took mental effort on Delgadito's part. He wanted to get it right. "Men of woods," he translated at last.

"Well, I've used Apache all my life, and that's what I'll go on using." Clay said his new name once. "The White Apache? Is that it?"

"Yes," Delgadito said, allowing the corners of his mouth to curl in a mocking smile.

Clay saw and mistook the smile for yet another friendly gesture. "I'm obliged. But I don't hardly live up to it. White Jackass would be more like it."

Such honesty confounded Delgadito. What sort of man would admit to such a thing? he asked himself as he rose. "We go. Much ground to cover."

"I'll do the best I can," Clay promised. The sleeves made a world of difference. After going so long without any footwear, it felt as if he was running on padded cushions. Sharp stones and cactus had to be avoided, as always, but on flat ground he experienced little pain at all.

Fatigue and hunger were other matters. Clay had
not eaten a full meal in days, nor had he fully
recuperated yet from the ordeal of the hanging and
his awful trek carrying Delgadito. When the posse
had been chasing him, the best he had managed
was to down a few pieces of jerky and to catch
fitful snatches of rest every now and then. Since
his hanging, all he'd had to eat was whatever concoction Delgadito's wife had given him, and the rest
he'd gotten had done little to refresh him. He felt
worn to a frazzle. Yet he dared not stop. The warrior
might leave him if he faltered, and he needed the
Apache's help to reach civilization.

At the first loud rumble from Clay's stomach,
Delgadito glanced over his shoulder but made no
comment. He was hungry too, but he had closed
his mind to his empty belly, just as he could close
his mind to pain and heat and thirst. This was yet
another example of how the Apaches were strong
and the Americans weak.

For an hour the pair trotted eastward, bathed by
the light of the steadily rising moon. Coyotes yipped
in the distance. Animals made rustling noises in the
brush. One time a bird squawked close at hand, followed by a flurry of flapping wings, then a louder,
shriller squawk that ended abruptly.

Clay wasn't as bothered by the darkness as he
would have been had he been alone amidst the
sprawling wilderness. A lone white man in Apache
country had to always be on his guard, despite
government assurances that the Apaches were no
longer much of a menace to life and limb and that
people could travel as freely as they wished. Being
with an Apache, however, and under that Apache's
protection, as Clay thought was the case, meant he
could relax to a degree he would have been unable
to do otherwise.

Delgadito stopped when he heard the white-eye huffing and puffing. He could have gone the rest of the night and most of the next day without a break—Apache men were able to cover up to 70 miles at one stretch—but he did not want to wear the American out, so for a short spell he sat and waited while Lickoyee-shis-inday recovered.

"Where are you taking me?" Clay asked between pants.

"Dragoons."

"To the reservation? Won't the Army find you?"

"We go secret place. Be safe while."

"Safe for *a* while," Clay corrected without thinking.

"I speak wrongly again?"

"You do it all the time, but it's nothing a little practice won't cure," Clay said. "I'm no stickler on grammar myself, but at least I can get by in a restaurant."

Delgadito had to wrestle with that word before he could say it. "A restaurant?"

"That's a highfalutin name for an eatery." Clay was breathing easier but not eager to go on just yet. He noticed a puzzled look on the Apache's face, and clarified by saying, "A fancy wickiup where whites belly up to the trough." Which, to his way of thinking, and in light of his sixth-grade education, was as precise as he could be.

But Delgadito was, if anything, more confused. He knew what a belly was, and he knew troughs were the big wooden vessels whites built for their horses to drink out of. There was no connection between the two, though, that he could see, especially in relation to whites eating. Once again the white tongue taunted him with a maze of meanings, and it bothered him more than ever that he couldn't speak the language of those he deemed inferiors.

"Tell you what," Clay said to keep the conversation going. "Since we're going to be together a spell, why don't you teach me Apache and I'll help you with your English. It'll help kill the time."

The idea was so novel that Delgadito showed surprise. When he had tried learning the tongue on the reservation, there had been no one to practice with. Few Apaches were versed in English, and the agent had been so busy all the time that Delgadito had found few opportunities to try out the words he had learned to see if he was saying them properly.

"What do you say?" Clay prompted.

The idea was appealing to Delgadito. Long ago, while perched on his father's knee, he had learned that the best way to overcome a foe was to know that foe as well as he knew himself. Whether those foes were Comanches, Maricopas, Mexicans, or Americans, knowledge of their ways was the key to defeating them. "We do that," he agreed, although doing so meant postponing his plan to make an example of the rancher.

"Good," Clay said. "Where do you want to start? How about if I point out things and give you their names in English, then you do the same in Apache?"

"Start later," Delgadito said, turning and trotting onward. "For now, much running."

"I was afraid you'd say that."

Clay wasn't accustomed to relying on his legs so much. As a rancher he had spent most of his daylight hours in the saddle and his evening hours behind his desk trying to make sense of his own scribble marks in his books. He walked from the house to the stable many times during a typical day, but that was a distance of one hundred feet. And running? Clay never, ever, did that, if no one counted the time he had been out on the range, gone into the bushes to answer Nature's call, and nearly squatted on top of a rattler. So his legs rebelled at such brutal treatment, and before another hour went by he was in utter torment. Yet still he trotted eastward.

No one could have been more amazed than Clay at his own persistence. He simply hadn't realized he had such grit because he had never been put to such a test before. There had been no denying he was tough, tough in the sense that most ranchers in the Southwest were tough, hardy souls who fought the harsh land and elements for the few dollars of profit they earned each year. And yes, he had known he was strong, physically strong, because he could lift two full kegs without straining a muscle. But no man knew if he had true grit until a true challenge came along, a challenge such as he now faced.

And there was another reason why Clay didn't stop, didn't give in to the demands of his body: he didn't care to show weakness in front of the warrior. All Clay's life he had heard about Apaches. How they could go for days without food or water, and cover more ground afoot faster than a horse. How they were men of iron, men who felt no pain, who endured any hardship without complaint. And here he was, running behind one of those iron men, and he'd be damned if he'd let the Apache know that Apaches were better than whites. He had something to prove, not only to himself, but on behalf of his own kind.

After a time the pain dulled. Clay trotted mechanically, pumping his arms and legs without consciously doing so. His surroundings became a blur. The only sounds he heard were the throbbing in his temples and the drumming of his soles on the ground.

Delgadito, however, was keenly aware of their surroundings. His eyes roved constantly, and he often cocked his head to better catch the faintest sounds.

In addition, he regularly sniffed the air, testing for scents as a bloodhound would. So it was that he first detected an odor familiar to him, one which caused him to veer to the southeast, the direction from which the wind was now blowing. He had gone a dozen feet when he looked back and saw the white man still jogging blindly to the east. "Lickoyee-shis-inday," Delgadito said sarcastically to himself, and hurried to catch Taggart.

Clay stopped when he felt a restraining hand on his arm. He had been breathing so heavily for so long that he continued to do so while standing still. Fatigue blurred his mind, and he didn't understand why the warrior now wanted him to go a different way, but he obeyed, plodding along on his last legs—literally.

The detour had caused Delgadito to lose the scent. He ran in a zigzag pattern in an effort to pick it up again, but the breeze had slackened. Not until he rounded another hill did he smell what he sought, and he saw, not far off, where the hills and the flatland merged, a tiny flicker of firelight. Such a small fire had to be the handiwork of Indians, perhaps some of his own people. He hurried, or tried to, but the rancher slowed him down.

Delgadito chafed at the delay. He wanted to be among his own again and to report the atrocity that had been committed. Once the word spread, other warriors might flock to his cause. He couldn't—he wouldn't—accept that he was the only Apache left unwilling to accept the reservation yoke.

In Delgadito's eagerness to see others of his tribe, he almost made a fatal blunder. He had approached within 40 yards of the fire when the flames flared just as a figure passed nearby, and in the spreading glow Delgadito could clearly see that the man wore the hated uniform of the U.S. Army.

Chapter Six

Clay Taggart was shuffling along in the Apache's wake, so exhausted he could barely think straight, when he saw the warrior suddenly flatten. Puzzled, he gazed beyond Delgadito and spied a soldier crouched by a fire, fanning the flames, and other soldiers rising from their blankets. He also saw an officer walking toward a string of horses.

Excited at seeing white men again, Clay forgot himself and opened his mouth wide to call out to them. He completely forgot about his run-in with Gillett and the horrible aftermath. No sounds came from his throat, though, for as his mouth opened he was seized and yanked to the ground. A palm covered with grains of dirt was pressed over his lips and the Apache's face loomed close to his.

"Do not make noise!"

Clay didn't want to anymore anyway. His head had cleared enough for him to realize a warrant might still be out for his arrest even though, so far as Marshal Crane knew, he was dead. That was because Crane hadn't had time to reach Tucson and cancel any warrants. Clay had to play it safe and not give himself away until he knew for sure he could do so without being thrown in the nearest jail.

The cavalry patrol was gearing up for another day. Troopers tended to the stock while others were busy rolling up their bedding. A husky corporal had coffee going. The officer, a young, energetic type whose spine was as stiff as a board, was everywhere, over-seeing operations.

Clay knew some of the officers at Fort Bowie thanks to his occasional visits there to sell beef, but not this one. The troops never seemed to have enough rations, perhaps because Fort Bowie was regarded as the armpit of the West, the post of last resort for has-beens, soldiers prone to causing trouble, and other sundry sorts the Army would not dearly miss should they fall prey to Apaches.

Clay wondered why this particular patrol was far-ther west than usual. Had the Army gotten word of Delgadito's band and sent out a force to try and cor-ral him? Or had the Army learned of Ben Johnson venturing north of the border?

The troopers were gathering for their cup of hot coffee and hardtack before mounting. Little was said, except by the busy officer, who reminded several of his men to adjust their uniforms. In due course the fire was extinguished, the men climbed onto their horses, and four abreast, the column rode eastward.

By then the sun crowned the distant Dragoons with vivid streaks of red, orange, and pink. Delgadito watched the cavalry leave with regret. The odor of horses had drawn him to the camp, and he had wanted to claim two of them for his own so he could reach the mountains that much faster. Now the journey would take the better part of the day, or even longer, depending on how well the white tortoise held up.

Which wasn't well at all. Clay stood when the warrior did and followed Delgadito eastward, but he hadn't gone over 50 yards when his exhaustion returned with a vengeance and he found he could barely plant one foot in front of the other. He tried, though, tried his utmost. To no avail.

The first inkling Delgadito had that he wouldn't be going very far came when he heard a thud and turned to find the white-eye sprawled senseless. Frowning, Delgadito walked back and roughly lifted the American. Again he was tempted to leave the man to burn in the sun, but he didn't. He hiked to a ravine, sought shelter in a thicket at its base, where he placed the rancher in the shade, and then went off to locate water.

Clay Taggart awakened shortly thereafter. He blinked in confusion, uncertain of where he was or what had happened until he looked down at himself and saw the breechcloth. "Delgadito?" he said, rising on an elbow. He was surprised to find himself in a thicket, and worried about the warrior's absence. There could only be one explanation, he figured. The Apache had tired of having him slow them down and had simply left him.

Sitting up, Clay took stock. He was hungry, tired, and thirsty. As much as he needed rest, his body needed nourishment more, nourishment he wouldn't find sitting there in that thicket. Clay stood, brushed his legs off, and worked his way through the thicket to the ravine floor. The sheer walls were intimidating, so he began walking, seeking a means of getting out.

Presently Clay came to the mouth of the ravine. Here he had a decision to make, an easy decision as it turned out since there was only one direction he could go and have any hope of staying alive. In the Dragoons were streams and game and trees offering shadowy havens from the heat, so he headed toward them, plodding painfully.

For some reason the exhaustion Clay had succumbed to earlier wasn't as severe, or so he thought. He attributed his newfound strength to the grit he had not known he had, and he flattered himself that he could go for miles yet before he'd need rest.

The truth, though, was that Clay Taggart had driven his battered body to its limits, and well beyond, farther than most men had ever driven theirs. He was at that point where his mind was numb to the pangs and aches in his body because his mind itself was numb from being pushed so far beyond the brink of human endurance.

So Clay plodded blithely on, the dark, inviting silhouettes of the Dragoons the beacon that lured him, inspired him, guided him. Only vaguely was he aware of the blazing sun on his back and shoulders; only vaguely did he note that his skin was becoming a striking shade of red.

And while Clay made for the mountains, Delgadito came to the thicket bearing a bowl-shaped rock containing water he had dug out of the ground at a promising spot. When he saw that the white man was gone, he looked around in disbelief and immediately spotted tracks that told him the whole story.

The rancher had run off on him! Delgadito gulped the water, threw the rock aside, and took up the trail. He was not to be so easily denied, not when he now had a useful purpose to which the American could be put. And too, he was annoyed Taggart had seen fit to go on alone after all Delgadito had done on the white man's behalf.

It didn't take long for Delgadito to overtake the American. Where Taggart was a tortoise, Delgadito was a hare. He covered half a mile and spied a weaving figure up ahead. Increasing his speed, he was a score of yards behind when Taggart stumbled and collapsed in a disjointed heap. In disgust, Delgadito stood over the unconscious man and kicked him once in the ribs. "You are worthless, white-eye," he said in his own tongue.

Clay Taggart was in a bad way. He had sweated so much he had wrung practically all the moisture from his body. His skin was beet red, except on the shoulders and upper back, where it was burnt to a blistered crisp. And blood showed on the tattered remnants of the sleeves covering his feet.

"I should let you die, worthless one," Delgadito grumbled. And he might have too, had not the same unwanted memory haunted him, the memory of this white man saving him from the scalp hunters. Delgadito had never been obligated to anyone before. He had always relied on his skill and strength to see him safely through any danger, and until the battle at the hollow they had sufficed. It bothered him that he owed his life to an enemy, yet at the same time in the depths of his being he could not bring himself to ignore such a debt.

Delgadito knelt, draped Clay Taggart over his left shoulder, and ran on, bearing the heavy body as if it was that of a small child, his stocky, bronzed frame showing no strain at all. For miles he ran, until the broiling inferno of early afternoon compelled him to halt in the only shaded nook he found, a narrow gully. There were limits beyond which even an Apache dared not go, and he had reached his.

Delgadito set the white man down and stood staring at the now-scarlet, swollen face. Apache boys spent so much time outdoors that by the age of seven

they were the hue of copper and as impervious to the
sun's rays as they were to frigid cold and blustery
winds. The weather ceased to be a factor in their
lives. Rain or shine, summer or winter, they were
at home in the wild.

Whites, Delgadito had learned, were the opposite.
When it rained, they sought dry shelters. When it
snowed, they sought warmth. In the desert they
could not last more than three days without a full
canteen at their side. And the sun roasted them alive
if they weren't careful. As Taggart hadn't been.

Delgadito scanned the barren landscape. The nearest water was a spring at the edge of the Dragoons, a
small spring known only to his people. If he rested
until nightfall, he could be there before the night
was a third done. But could the white-eye hold out
that long?

Taking a seat, Delgadito touched Taggart's brow
and found it far too hot. The man needed mending,
of that there was no doubt. But there was little
Delgadito could do. He was a warrior, after all.
His wife, an expert in such matters, had taught
him enough for him to mend himself when on a
raid. He knew of certain herbs that might reduce
the fever, but to obtain them meant roving around
during the worst part of the day, which Delgadito
flatly refused to do. He owed the white man for his
life, but he wouldn't give his own to pay his debt. Not
when there were so many other whites he intended
to kill.

Leaning back, Delgadito lowered his chin to his
muscular chest, closed his eyes, and was instantly
asleep. This was another Apache trait, ingrained
by constant practice. On a raid a warrior had to
be able to snatch what rest he could whenever he
could. Being able to drift off at a moment's notice
often meant the difference between being refreshed

for a battle or having to fight while one's senses were sluggish, which might prove fatal.

Although Delgadito slept, his senses didn't. He heard Taggart's occasional groans. He heard the beating of bird wings when one passed overhead. And he heard a lizard scuttle past. The latter brought him around, but the lizard disappeared before he could spot it. Ignoring his growling stomach, he fell back asleep.

The sun traversed the bright blue sky and bid the world good night. No sooner had it sunk from view than Delgadito awoke a second time, rose, and stretched. Once more Taggart went over his shoulder. He resumed his tireless dogtrot, alert for whatever sounds the wind brought him.

The mournful wail of a coyote reminded Delgadito of his own sorrow. He had lost many friends and relatives over the years, to Americans, Mexicans, and other tribes alike, but none could match the loss of his family, of his own band. They had trusted him, had fled with him from the reservation because they believed his promise of a better life. They had shared his vision of a sanctuary where the long arm of the U.S. Army couldn't reach.

And look at what had happened! Pure rage welled up within Delgadito, rage such as he had never known, rage so potent it was more intoxicating than *tizwin*. Before the loss of his band he had hated Americans, yes, but not like now. He wanted to crush them all, to slay every last one in Apache territory.

Delgadito was a realist. A lone warrior could accomplish little, but he would do the best he was able. He would harass the Army at every opportunity, waylay lone travelers, and attack the stage on occasion. He would be such a thorn in the side of the Americans that they would sit up and take notice and say among themselves, "There is one true Apache left!"

Oddly enough, at that moment Delgadito remembered the look of baffled rage and hatred he had seen on Clay Taggart's face when the rancher had been hung by the posse. They had something in common, then, the white-eye and himself. They both had someone to hate. They both craved revenge.

Such musings occupied Delgadito until he was close enough to the mountains to smell the scent of water. A gorge drew him like a magnet, and once between its towering ramparts he went directly to a certain fissure. Beyond was an opening clear to the top and in it the spring.

Delgadito splashed water on the rancher's face, but Taggart only groaned louder and fluttered his eyes. The man was ill, very ill, and might not last much longer. All Delgadito had to do was leave for a day and let Nature take its course. He didn't, though. Instead Delgadito cooled Taggart from head to toe with water and poured handfuls down Taggart's throat.

The soothing sensation brought Clay partially around. He figured he must be dreaming until he swallowed and tasted water so delicious as to be indescribable. Greedily, he gulped more. He opened his eyes and glimpsed a patch of stars far overhead. Closer loomed Delgadito's head. "You!" Clay said, unable to get over his amazement at how decently the warrior was treating him.

"No talk. You very sick."

"Where are we?"

"Dragoons."

"So soon?"

"Long time getting here."

"I'm obliged for all you've done," Clay said. He wanted to say more, but his fever flared and emptiness engulfed him. When next he opened his eyes, he was alone, on his back. Moonlight filtered from on high, relieving the oppressive darkness. Propping an arm as a support, he sat up and saw a spring on his right.

"Thank God," Clay breathed, lowering his lips to the surface and gulping. He couldn't seem to get enough. His body was so overheated that no matter how much he drank, he needed more. Although he knew better, he drank and drank until his stomach hurt and he had to stop or suffer worse consequences.

Clay rolled onto his back and rested. The simple act of drinking had fatigued him so much he knew he was in a bad way. His shoulder started itching, so he reached up to scratch. The instant his fingers touched his skin he was racked by the most intense pain imaginable. Stunned, he probed along his upper back, which added to his agony but showed he was suffering from severe sunburn.

"If it isn't one damn thing, it's another," Clay groused. He soothed the sunburn with water, and when the pain had gone away he reluctantly sat up to check his feet. The sleeves were no longer there. Many of the blisters had broken. Some of the flesh was so raw to the touch that he couldn't bear the thought of how his soles would look in broad daylight. He wanted to dip both feet in the spring, but was wise enough to know that doing so might taint the water.

Suddenly Clay had the feeling that he was being watched. Glancing up, he spotted a crack in the rock wall, and framed in the opening was a husky figure. "Delgadito," he said. "Where the hell did you

get to? I hope you've brought something to eat. I'm
half starved."

The figure advanced, and behind it came another,
and another. Into the moonlight they strode, fanning
out to block the entrance. Their features were impassive but there was no denying the glittering hatred
in their flinty eyes. All three were Apaches.

Clay was dumbfounded. He had no idea whether
the trio were from Delgadito's band or another. How
he wished he had taken the time to learn a few
Apache words from Delgadito, at least enough to
offer a friendly greeting! To show them his peaceful intentions, he smiled broadly and said, "Howdy.
There's enough water here for all of us if you're
thirsty."

They made no response. They just stared. At length
the warrior in the middle spoke in their tongue and
started to draw the knife on his hip.

"Now hold on," Clay said. "I don't mean you any
harm. Do you understand? Do you savvy English?"
Apparently they didn't, because the next second the
others seized him and hoisted him roughly to his feet
while the Apache holding the knife waved the blade
in small circles and grinned in anticipation. "I'm not
your enemy, damn you!" Clay shouted, struggling
feebly. He flinched when the tip of the blade pricked
his chin, then raised his head defiantly and glared at
the brave. Weak as he was, he wasn't about to grovel.
If it was his time to die, he'd die like a man.

The knife-wielder said something to the others,
raised his weapon high overhead, and tensed.

It was at that moment Delgadito returned carrying a rabbit he had slain. At sight of the three
warriors he called out "No!" in their tongue and
hurried forward. The three shifted and regarded him
coldly. "I do not want him killed yet," he informed
them.

Cuchillo Negro reluctantly lowered his knife and said, "It is good to see you alive, Delgadito. We thought we were the only ones who escaped."

Delgadito stared at Amarillo and Ponce until they let go of the American, who slumped to his knees and clutched at his sunburnt arms. "And I believed I was the only one," he said.

"There may be a few more," Cuchillo Negro declared. "But not many. The scalp hunters were very thorough." Only another Apache could have read the deep sorrow in his impassive face or detected the sadness in his tone.

"We are heading for the secret place," Amarillo said. "We knew if anyone else lived, they would head there too."

The youngest warrior, Ponce, was staring resentfully at the white-eye and fingering the knife at his belt. "Why do you keep this dog with you, Delgadito? Did you not see the whites among those who destroyed our band? Did you not see the one they call Blue Cap, their leader, himself a white?"

"I saw."

"And you have allowed this *Americano* to live?" Ponce said in disgust. "He deserves the same death our people got. Give him to me and I will make him scream for his life before I take his hair."

"Not yet," Delgadito insisted, and was given hard looks by all three. He knew they now doubted his judgment. In light of what had happened, he couldn't blame them for doing so. But old habits were slow to die. For the time being he was still the leader of their band even though there was no longer any band to lead, and they would do as he wanted for a while yet. Eventually, though, one would see fit to dispute him, and how he reacted would decide his future standing among them.

"Wagh!" Ponce said, which was the Apache way of showing extreme anger. Turning, he stalked to the spring and knelt to drink. Amarillo joined him.

Cuchillo Negro stayed where he was, his eyes conveying his feelings more eloquently than words.

"Trust me," Delgadito said.

"I always have. We all have. And look at where it has gotten us."

"Do you think I do not hurt inside? Do you think I do not want to gut myself and let the lizards eat my intestines? I would, if there was not something else I must do." Delgadito dropped the limp rabbit and sat. "I will never be the same again."

"None of us will," Cuchillo Negro said. "None of us will be men again until we have avenged the loss of our families." He took a seat next to his friend. "You know what must be done."

"I do."

"When?"

"When it is time."

"Will you go before the council and ask for help?"

"No."

"But we are too few."

Delgadito had drawn the Bowie knife and started skinning the rabbit. "Palacio would speak out against us and say we brought our fate on ourselves by leaving the reservation. He would say our fight is our own, and that no more lives should be wasted over a lost cause. And he would be right."

"How can you say that?"

"Because I now know his way *is* the right way for Shis-Inday who have wives and children. Had I listened to him and the other chiefs, had I stayed where the whites wanted me to stay, all those we cared for would still be alive." The Bowie slipped, nicking Delgadito's thumb. He idly raised it to his lips and licked off a drop of blood. "Perhaps some-times it is better to bend with the wind than to be broken by it."

"I cannot believe I hear you saying these words," Cuchillo Negro responded. "You were the one who put fire in our veins, who convinced us freedom was better than slavery, who taught us that we should live as our people have always lived and not as miserable farmers."

The words seared into Delgadito's conscience like a red-hot coal, and he applied himself to the rabbit rather than respond. He didn't need to be reminded that he and he alone was responsible for the loss of so many. He and he alone must bear the burden of blame.

Not a yard away, Clay Taggart ran a palm over his right shoulder and wished he was able to understand Apache. Being left in the dark made him uneasy. For all he knew they might be discussing how to dispose of him. Any fool could see that the three newcomers didn't care for him one whit. The pair by the spring, in fact, hadn't stopped glaring at him from the moment he'd seen them. He suspected that if he turned his back on them at the wrong time, he'd end up with steel between his shoulders.

Clay glanced at the opening and debated whether to make a run for it. For two reasons he didn't. He knew he wouldn't get ten feet, and he also knew that despite everything, despite his condition and the hatred of the other Apaches, he was better off with Delgadito than he'd be on his own. At least until he was on the mend and could rustle up his own food. That would be when he'd slip away and head for a settlement.

How long would it be, though? Clay wondered. Every moment spent with the Apaches was another moment he cheated death. And no man's luck lasted forever. Grunting, he moved to the pool and splashed more water on his aching shoulders and back. The chilling stares of the nearby Apaches added to the goose flesh that broke out all over him.

Be patient, Clay told himself. He'd get his chance. Sooner or later, he would escape, and if the Apaches tried to stop him, he'd sell his life dearly.

He just hoped it wouldn't come to that.

Chapter Seven

For the next two days Clay Taggart traveled deeper into the Chiricahua Reservation with the four Apaches. How he kept up, he would never know. Delgadito made a poultice that helped with the sunburn. And his feet, after a while, no longer hurt. Yet still he was hard pressed not to fall behind since the Apaches maintained a pace that would have tired a thoroughbred. Or a mountain goat, which was a closer comparison. Clay was continually amazed at their uncanny ability to cover the most rugged terrain as effortlessly as if they were strolling through a city park. Somehow, some way, they always took the path of least resistance, as wild animals would do.

Clay studied them, and he learned without quite realizing how much he was learning. For instance, he learned to take shorter steps instead of long strides to conserve his energy. He learned to put more weight on the balls of his feet rather than the heels, which was less tiring over long distances. He also acquired the knack of breathing deeply while on the go, which made a lengthy trek easier for his body to bear.

And there was more. Delgadito taught Clay how to carry a mouthful of water in his mouth for miles, swallowing bit by bit until the water was gone. Delgadito showed how to use a pebble to take the place of water by keeping it in the mouth for long periods, which made the mouth salivate. And Delgadito showed which cactus were good sources of water and which weren't.

For Clay's part, he was as good as his word and taught the Apache English every chance he had. At the same time, Delgadito imparted his own tongue. Since both of them were anxious to learn for very separate reasons, they made swift progress.

On the fourth day after entering the Dragoons, they had climbed high into the mountains, up where the stark peaks were silhouetted against the blue sky and hawks soared on outstretched wings. And it was here that Clay nearly lost his life.

Toward evening the Apaches stopped on a shelf watered by a sluggish creek, actually no more than a trickle six inches wide. They went off to hunt, leaving Clay to get the fire going as Delgadito had trained him to do. Clay had busily gathered brush, and had just climbed back to the shelf with his arms heavily laden when he saw a warrior standing a few feet away, facing in the opposite direction.

"Delgadito?" Clay asked, since the warrior's build was about the same. "Get any game?"

The warrior stiffened and whirled, his hand streaking to his knife.

With a start, Clay saw that this was a new Apache, a warrior he didn't recall ever seeing before, a man with a hawkish face, fiery eyes, and a nasty fresh wound on his brow, a wound that would leave a scar in the shape of a lightning bolt when it healed. The brave was heavily muscled, perhaps even more so than Delgadito, and those muscles rippled as he drew his knife and crouched.

"Nejeunee!" Clay exclaimed, the Apache word for "friend," as he dropped the firewood and held out his hands to show he had no hostile intentions. But the advancing warrior paid no heed. Hissing like a serpent, he wagged his knife and closed for the kill.

Clay was in a tight fix. He was at the very edge of the shelf and couldn't very well retreat. Nor was there much room to maneuver on either side because the shelf curved. He glanced around for something he could use as a weapon, but there was nothing other than a few small stones and the pile of wood he had gathered. With no other recourse, he grabbed a stout broken limb and edged to the left, away from the warrior. His mind raced as he tried to think of other Apache words that would show he wasn't an enemy, but in the excitement of the moment his mind was blank.

Had Clay known the mood of the Apache facing him, he would have realized that reasoning with the warrior was pointless. For the brave with the fresh scar was none other than Fiero, who had revived hot and feverish on the baking plain the day after he had been shot and found El Chico staked out, skinned, and mutilated. Weak from his infected wound, Fiero had tried to hurry back to the hollow to warn his people. Countless times he had passed out and collapsed, only to rise hours later and press on. The journey had taxed him to the limit, and he might have perished had he not been able to kill a snake on the second day and fill his belly with its raw meat.

When Fiero reached the encampment and found the butchered bodies and the burned wickiups, his rage was boundless. He had no wife, no children, because none of the women would have anything to do with a man of such raw temper, but the slaughter affected him as deeply as it had Delgadito and Cuchillo Negro because those slaughtered were *Apaches*, were Fiero's own people, those he had known and lived among since childhood.

Fiero spent a full day there reading the sign and memorizing every hoofprint and boot and moccasin track. He had a memory for tracks, and he knew that one day he would come across some made by those who took part in the attack, and he would be able to repay them in kind for the destruction of the band.

From the hollow Fiero had headed eastward toward the Dragoons simply because he had nowhere else to go. Other Apaches were in the mountains, reservation Apaches but still Apaches, and he wanted the company of his own kind. Presently he came across strange sign that puzzled him greatly. There were two sets of tracks, one those of a barefoot white man, the other those of an Apache. At first Fiero thought the Apache was stalking the white-eye, but later it became apparent the two were traveling together, and at times the Apache was actually helping the white along.

Still later, Fiero learned that three other warriors had joined the pair. His sickness had nearly gone away by then and he'd hurried to overtake the party. Now, on this shelf, he had found where the warriors had separated to hunt, and he had been trying to decide whether to wait for them to return or to go after one of them when he heard the voice of a hated white and he turned to find one of his enemies ten feet away.

It mattered not to Fiero that this white man had been in the company of fellow Apaches. And while it had occurred to him earlier that the American might be the same one Delgadito had brought to camp, when he set eyes on the man, the only thought Fiero had was to kill. His rage eclipsed all else.

Clay Taggart saw the warrior tense his legs, and did the same. When the scarred fury hurtled at him, Clay hurled himself to one side. The knife gleamed in the sunlight, narrowly missing his chest. He countered by clubbing the branch at the warrior's head, but the man skipped lightly aside. Then they stood and stared, each taking the other's measure.

Clay didn't like what he saw. The Apache's ugly face was made uglier by his hatred, a hatred so strong Clay could almost feel it. The branch, although bigger than the knife, seemed a puny defense against a razor-sharp blade. *"Nejeunee!"* he tried again.

For a white-eye to claim to be a friend was more than Fiero could bear. He sprang, his knife going for a neck cut, but the American scrambled backward and blocked it with the branch. Fiero pressed his attack, thrusting high and low, seeking an opening.

Clay was only able to keep the Apache at bay because the limb was longer. He countered thrust after thrust, retreating the whole while, until suddenly he came to where a slope rose upward from the shelf and he could go no further. He darted to the left, or tried to, but the Apache was on him in a twinkling.

A sheer accident saved Clay's life. He tripped as he was raising the branch, and as he started to fall the knife speared at his throat but hit the branch instead, hit and stuck fast, imbedded several inches in the wood. Before he could take advantage of the warrior's mistake, he was flat on his back with the warrior astride him. The only thing keeping the Apache from his throat was the branch, which the warrior was trying to wrest from his grasp.

Fiero was fighting by sheer instinct. When he was in one of his periodic rages, all conscious thought deserted him. He lived for only one purpose: to kill, to rip, to tear. There were times when such wild behavior worked in his favor and other times, such as now, when his own blind fury prevented him from doing what he most wanted to do. For had he thought to yank the knife from the branch, he would have easily slain his enemy. Instead, he became intent on getting his hands around the other's throat to the exclusion of all else.

Clay knocked the warrior's grasping fingers to one side, drove the blunt end of his branch into the Apache's chest, and then slammed the branch into the man's temple. The Apache fell off, allowing Clay to scramble to his feet. A foot flicked at his knee, glancing off it as he jerked backward, causing pain but not so much that he couldn't keep on fighting. He swung at the warrior's head.

Fiero ducked underneath the limb and pushed upright. He was unarmed but still deadly. His bulging muscles attested to his great strength, which he had used on more than one occasion to break the spine of a foe or to choke an adversary to death. He sneered in contempt at the white-eye as he circled, his hands held low, his thick fingers flexing and unflexing.

Clay Taggart had never longed for anything as much as he did for Delgadito to return. But this time he was on his own, his fate in his own hands. He feinted, feinted again, forcing the Apache back toward the edge of the shelf. A harebrained idea made him persist, lancing the branch again and again, never quite connecting but always driving the warrior further and further back. He expected the Apache to realize what he was up to, and he was more than a little surprised when he was able to force the warrior to the very brink.

Fiero awakened to his danger too late. His heel brushed the edge, alerting him. He glanced back, tried to throw himself to the right, and in so doing left his side exposed. The branch caught him flush in the ribs, knocking him off balance, over the brink. He attempted a flip to stay on the shelf, but without a firm purchase it was hopeless.

A laugh burst from Clay as he watched the Apache tumble downward, a laugh of relief, not triumph. He knew the warrior would come right back up after him, and he had a hand on the knife hilt to try to pull it loose when the Apache smashed into a boulder with a loud thud. The warrior got to his hands and knees, his face all bloody, and glowered up at Clay. Two steps the Apache took, two steps, and then he pitched forward and was still.

Clay gulped. He lowered the branch to the ground, placed a foot on it to hold it in place, and wrenched at the knife until the blade was loose. Down the slope he bounded to where the Apache was sprawled. Squatting, he seized the warrior's hair and turned the head so the throat was visible. He raised the knife, then paused.

How would Delgadito react if he killed an Apache? Clay asked himself. Delgadito was the only friend he had, the one keeping the other warriors from slaying him. If he did anything that turned Delgadito against him, Delgadito might let the others have their way. He wavered, his clenched hand trembling from the intensity of his feeling. "Damn it all!" he snapped, and lowered his arm.

When Delgadito and Cuchillo Negro returned bearing a dead buck, they were amazed to see Fiero on his back beside the fire and the American seated next to him.

Clay jumped up, nodded at the unconscious warrior, and explained, "He attacked me."

No one had ever beaten Fiero. Delgadito had doubted even *he* could. It shocked him as few things ever had to behold the fiercest Apache of them all laid low by the weak white-eye, and in his shock he blurted out in awe, "Lickoyee-shis-inday."

Cuchillo Negro glanced at him but made no comment.

"I tried to tell him I was a friend," Clay went on. "*Nejeunee.* Isn't that the right word? I told him that, twice, but he wouldn't listen. Did I say it wrong?"

Letting the buck drop, Delgadito walked up to Fiero, whose chest was rhythmically rising and falling. Blood seeped from a wicked wound, and there was another, older wound, a bullet crease. "How you do this?" he asked.

"He fell."

"Fell?"

"Hit his head on a boulder. Any harder and he would've split his noggin right open." Clay fidgeted, unable to judge from Delgadito's expression whether Delgadito was angry or not. "He was trying to kill me. I didn't have any choice but to protect myself."

"You protect very well."

"No hard feelings, right? I mean, I don't want you getting your dander up on account of this. We're still friends, aren't we?"

The question was so preposterous that Delgadito looked at Clay, thinking it was a joke. Apaches and whites could never be friends, not after the great deception. Americans had come to Apache territory speaking words of peace and friendship, when all the time the Americans had planned to conquer all Apaches and take Apache land as their own. The words of the whites were as false as the many promises made by the Great White Father. Conquerors and conquered, that was their relationship. Bitter enemies until the end of time.

But when Delgadito stared at Clay Taggart, he saw that the white man was serious, and that Taggart placed value on their assumed friendship. Which was amusing. Among Apaches themselves deep friendships were rare because every warrior was always looking out for his own interests.

"We are still friends, aren't we?" Clay persisted. "You're not fixing to hold this against me?"

"We the same," Delgadito assured him, which was true in that he had not changed his mind about making a lesson of the rancher when he was done using him.

Clay exhaled and held out the knife. "Here. You'd better take this. He'll be fit to spit nails if he sees me holding it when he comes to."

"You not kill him. Why?"

"I didn't have call to."

Delgadito sensed the white man was being evasive. "Why?" he pressed him. "He try kill you. You say so."

"I could have slit his throat," Clay admitted, "but I didn't. I didn't want to get on your bad side."

Here was something new. The American so valued their friendship that he had spared the life of a man trying to kill him. Delgadito did not know what to make of such strange behavior, and he was annoyed at himself because he felt a certain slight fondness for Taggart for what the man had done. Keeping his feelings to himself, he squatted. "Stand back," he advised, and gave Fiero a ringing slap.

As if shot from the ground, Fiero sat up and looked around. "Delgadito," he said in greeting. Then he laid eyes on the white man and he began to rise, the veins in his neck bulging. "Him! I will rip out his heart—"

"You will not," Delgadito interrupted, grabbing Fiero's arm. "We need him."

Fiero yanked free. "You go too far. You no longer have the right to advise us what to do. I no longer acknowledge you as our leader."

Delgadito folded his arms. This was the challenge he had expected, but from one he had no longer expected to make it. He had believed Fiero to be dead, and now Fiero had come back from the grave to be the same thorn in his side he had always been. "You are right," Delgadito said, and was gratified by the surprise the other showed. "After what has happened, I can only hang my head in shame. No one should heed my counsel, for my counsel has been proven wrong and those who depended on it have been slaughtered by Blue Cap."

Fiero grunted.

"I will never again lead any Shis-Inday," Delgadito went on. "I will never again let anyone do as I think best. Each of you must choose his own path."

"I could have told you what would happen," Fiero said arrogantly. "You were too timid. We should never have fled from the scalp hunters when we were in Mexico. Had we pushed on, our people would be alive."

While Delgadito was willing to accept blame for the loss of their band, he would not let anyone rub his nose in it. "I have accepted the fault as mine," he said testily. "No other words are necessary."

"And this white filth?" Fiero asked, jerking a thumb at Clay Taggart.

"He is with me."

"He is our *enemy*."

"An enemy who stayed his hand when he could have slain you. You owe him your life."

"I owe him nothing! He is a fool if he did not kill me when he had the chance because I will surely kill him just as soon as it pleases me to do so."

"Lickoyee shis-inday is under my care," Delgadito warned. "Harm him and you will answer to me."

"What did you call him?"

"The name I have given him."

"You—!" Fiero began, and stopped because he was so choked with fury that he could not speak. To befriend a white man was bad enough. To bestow an Apache name on one was the ultimate indignity. Fiero had to turn away and bite his lower lip to keep from saying something that would have brought Delgadito's knife streaking out.

As much as Fiero disliked Delgadito and thought the latter to be weak, Fiero had no desire to kill him. Slaying another Apache was taboo unless done during tribal warfare or during a proper duel when one warrior had issued a public challenge to another, and for such a challenge to be deemed appropriate the affront to the offended party had to be great. This was a result of the lesson learned during the old days, when so many duels were fought that the ranks of able-bodied warriors were gravely depleted.

In addition, Fiero would not kill Delgadito because despite his combative nature Fiero was passionately devoted to his tribe. Yes, he would argue with anyone and everyone when he felt they were wrong. Yes, he would bristle at the vaguest of slights. But deep down he was as devoted to his people as Cochise had been.

Fiero had long secretly harbored the dream of becoming a warrior of great influence, perhaps a leader of his own band. It had been his misfortune not to be born the son of a chief so he could one day inherit the mantle of leadership. The only way for him to acquire such coveted status was to earn it. And since wresting leadership from a weak rival was easier than from a strong one, Fiero had joined Delgadito's band.

Now Fiero's dreams were dashed. The band he had hoped to one day call his own had been wiped out. He could try to join another band, but the taint he brought with him would limit his chances at leadership. The taint put on him by Delgadito's foolishness.

Composing himself, Fiero faced around and said sarcastically, "Will you make this white-eye your brother too? Will the two of you share the same wickiup?"

"I have a use for him. When he has served that purpose, and not before, he will die."

Fiero looked into the other's eyes. This news was unexpected, and it showed, once again, that the threads of Delgadito's thoughts were hard to unravel. "What are you planning?" he bluntly asked.

"What would you do if you were me?"

There was only one answer. "I would wage war on all those who have invaded our land, and I would fight on until I drove them out or they took my life."

"A true Shis-Inday could do no less."

The seed of newfound respect for Delgadito took root in Fiero and he leaned forward excitedly. "I will join you."

"I no longer lead others."

"We will fight side by side then."

Cuchillo Negro, who had been listening attentively, came closer. "And I too will wage war on the white-eyes and the *nakai-hay*."

"I will not lead you either," Delgadito said.

Fiero and Cuchillo Negro exchanged puzzled glances.

"No one has to lead," the latter declared.

"Can a body move without a head? A band must have a leader to be effective," Delgadito said. "Even a small band of four or five warriors must have one who makes decisions or the band can not fight effectively. We would always be arguing among ourselves as to what we should do and when and we would never accomplish a thing."

"Then one of us will lead," Fiero said.

"Who? You?"

"Fiero is too hot-tempered to be a good leader," Cuchillo Negro quickly said. "I would not follow him, and neither would Ponce or Amarillo."

Predictably, Fiero bristled. "I would make as good a leader as any of you. Better, since I am not afraid to take the risks others shy away from."

Delgadito was staring thoughtfully at the ground. "Being capable is not enough. One must be able to attract followers before one can lead."

"Who will lead us if not you or I?" Fiero snapped. "The others are too young. They do not have our experience. Do you have someone else in mind?"

"No," Delgadito lied, his gaze idly roving over the mountainous terrain to the east, over a nearby peak, and over the shelf itself, finally coming to rest on Lickoyee-shis-inday. And had either Fiero or Cuchillo Negro been watching him closely, they would have seen the corners of Delgadito's mouth twitch upward.

Chapter Eight

Warm Springs, the Apaches called it, a natural fortress located high in the Chiricahua Mountains, one of the two ranges forming the backbone of the Chiricahua Reservation. There was just one way in or out, through a narrow cleft in a cliff. Inside, a narrow grassy valley afforded an ideal hiding place, ringed as it was by towering, unscalable rocky heights. Only the Chiricahuas knew of its existence. They had never told anyone outside their tribe about it, not even anyone from another Apache tribe. It was one of their most zealously guarded secrets.

So it was that Fiero, Ponce, and Amarillo argued heatedly against allowing Lickoyee-shis-inday to enter the refuge. To all their protests, Delgadito responded that they needed somewhere to lay low for a while and there was no better spot in all of Arizona. He noted that others might have survived the massacre, and if so, Warms Springs was where they would eventually come. If no one arrived within half a moon, then Delgadito would go elsewhere. Fiero, Ponce, and Amarillo reluctantly agreed to wait there that long for the sake of any survivors.

Clay Taggart guessed that he was the reason for the many arguments he witnessed, an easy guess to make in light of the frequent glares shot his way by three of the warriors. He had progressed enough in learning the Apache tongue to enable him to catch occasional words here and there, so it was plain to him that all three wanted him dead. More fully than ever he realized his life was in Delgadito's hands, and if anything should happen to Delgadito, his fate would be sealed.

Clay began to regret tagging along with the Apache. In his estimation he would have been better off on his own, even if he had to face the specter of starvation or dying of thirst. He became eager to get clear of the band, but he saw no way of doing so since he doubted they would just let him walk off on his own. It occurred to him that maybe the Apaches were afraid he would report the hideaway to the Army, so on the sixth day of their stay he broached the subject to Delgadito by saying, "This is some hideout you have here. I don't see how you can find it again once you leave. I know I couldn't."

"Plenty safe here," the warrior responded. "But not safe enough."

"How so?"

"Chiricahua Army scouts know Warm Springs. So far they not tell."

As Clay knew, Apaches from several tribes had signed on to work for the government in various capacities. A few worked for the agent. Others, those who couldn't abide the dull reservation life, had donned Army uniforms and became scouts. It was the only job an Apache could take that promised some adventure and excitement.

"One day one will," Delgadito had gone on. "Then Warm Springs not safe again."

"I'd never tell," Clay declared. "Not after all you've done for me."

Delgadito sat staring into the distance.

"No, sir," Clay stressed. "I'm not no tinhorn. When I give my word, you can count on me keeping it. If you were to let me go, your secret would be safe with me." He looked at the Apache, hoping Delgadito would take the hint and talk about allowing him to leave, but the warrior simply sat there, inscrutable as ever. Exasperated, Clay made bold to ask, "When the hell can I go anyway? I don't aim to stay here forever."

"Where you go?" Delgadito inquired mildly.

"I don't rightly know. I haven't got my plans all worked out yet. Maybe to my ranch first to get my poke and some clothes and guns."

"And after?"

"Then I reckon I'd look up the man responsible for my hanging and give him a taste of his own medicine." The mere thought of Gillett brought a flush of anger to Clay's cheeks. It had been days since he last pondered revenge, but his feelings had not changed one bit. If anything, they were stronger, and all his hatred returned in a rush, the intensity of his emotion causing him to clench his fists until his knuckles were white.

"The man wearing badge?" Delgadito asked.

"Marshal Crane? I'd like to blow out his lamp, sure enough, but he's just an errand boy for Miles Gillett. Gillett's the hombre I really want!"

"How you kill him?"

"How else? I'll call him out and put windows in his skull."

"What?"

"I'll shoot him full of holes."

"And the others? The ones who put rope on neck?"

"I owe them too."

"You kill all?"

"Every last son of a bitch among them. They were vigilantes, nothing more. I didn't get a trial. No jury heard my case. Gillett wanted me dead, so he had them do his dirty work." Clay scowled. "I'll bet they lied when they got back to Tucson. I'll bet they spread the story that I was shot resisting arrest. That way, no one could accuse them of an illegal lynching."

"*Nah-kee-sah-tah*," Delgadito said.

"So what if there's twelve of them?" Clay responded. "No one can stand up to a man who's in the right and keeps on coming. If there's any justice in this loco world of ours, I'll get them all before the law makes wolf meat of me."

"*Nah-kee-sah-tah*," Delgadito repeated slowly. "Too many for you alone."

"A man does what he has to do," Clay said with a shrug.

"You have friends help?"

"Afraid not. I've always been something of a loner, going my own way when the common herd went another. There are a few men I'd call pards, but none that would have the gumption to stand up to the likes of Miles Gillett." Clay remembered Jacoby and Hesket and his face hardened. "There isn't anyone anywhere I can trust." He glanced at the warrior, cracked a grin, and put his hand on Delgadito's shoulder. "Except you. Don't that beat all? The only damn friend I have, and you're an Apache."

A crafty gleam came into Delgadito's eyes, a gleam he hid by shifting to gaze at a flock of sparrows. "You need help kill so many."

"Where would I find any help?" Clay said, and laughed bitterly. "No, I'm on my own."

"We help, maybe."

"You?"

"We help you, you help us."

This was a notion Clay had not even considered, and the thought was so startling that he stiffened as if bitten by a Gila monster. Mental pictures of the Apaches swooping down on the ranches of those who had hanged him made him tingle with anticipation. He could think of no more fitting end for the bastards than to have them butchered and scalped! Better yet, if the Apaches took the blame, no one would hold him accountable later on when he went back to reclaim his ranch and take up his life where he had left off. He chuckled in delight.

"You like?"

"I like very much," Clay confessed. "But what about your friends? They'd do that for me? The way they've been treating me, I figure they'd rather slit my throat than do me a favor."

"We see," Delgadito said, rising. He made for the spring, near which the four braves were seated. Except for Cuchillo Negro, they rarely spoke to him now, so incensed were they over the rancher being there. Delgadito deliberately ignored them as he knelt and drank. On sitting up, he said, most casually, "I have decided. I go on the warpath against the whites if none of our people show after eight sleeps."

"By yourself you do this?" Fiero asked.

"No."

"So you have changed your mind and want us to join you?" Cuchillo Negro inquired.

"No."

There was silence as they mulled over the implications of his answers. It was the impatient Fiero who voiced the crucial question. "If you do not want us, then who will you go on the warpath with? Warriors from the reservation?"

"No," Delgadito said. He dipped a hand in the water and ran his moist palm over his throat and his brow. Although outwardly impassive, inwardly he churned with excitement at the deception he was playing.

"Then who?" asked Ponce.

Delgadito's pause was masterful. "Lickoyee-shis-inday and I will make war together." Standing, he started to walk off, but Cuchillo Negro spoke his name.

"My ears must not hear as well as they once did. You and the white-eye are going to make war on other whites?"

"Yes."

"Who ever heard of an *Americano* making war on other *Americanos?*" Amarillo said.

"Remember the great war between the blue caps and the gray caps?" Delgadito reminded them. "The war we heard so much about from the agent and the other whites here on the reservation? Whites do fight whites when they have cause, and Lickoyee-shis-inday has plenty of cause."

"You lead a single white against their whole Army?" Fiero's voice was caustic.

"I told you once before," Delgadito answered. "I will never lead anyone again."

"You fight as brothers, you and this White Apache?" Amarillo said scornfully.

Here was the critical moment. "No," Delgadito replied. "I will follow, he will lead." Turning, he walked off and sat on a flat boulder situated in the shade of an overhang on the rock wall. Leaning back, he closed his eyes, or pretended to, so he could watch the four men without being seen. As he expected, they were in an animated discussion over his disclosure. Hiding his grin, he shut his eyes fully and relaxed. Soon one of them or all of them would come to him, and then would his *na-tse-kes* bear its fruit.

Among Apaches, he who wielded the greatest influence was invariably he who was the deepest thinker, the one whose carefully laid plans reached far into the future and took into account all that might arise to affect his plans. Such men were highly regarded by all the tribe, and by the cleverness of their thoughts they were able to collect about them large bands of devoted warriors and their families. In this manner Delgadito had gathered his own band, and while most of his band was now gone, he was still a firm believer in *na-tse-kes*, in deep thinking.

This was the important difference between Delgadito and Fiero and the reason the latter would never rise higher than being a war chief. That in itself was quite an honor, but a war chief was not as esteemed as one who had proven his ability as a natural leader in all respects. Fiero, whose thinking ran as shallow as a stream during the summer, could aspire to higher influence all he wanted, but it would forever be denied him. He simply did not know how to use his mind properly.

Such were Delgadito's thoughts when he heard their footfalls and opened his eyes to find all four of them standing in front of him. "You want something?"

"What do you hope to gain from joining White Apache in this war?" Cuchillo Negro asked him.

"Revenge for the deaths of those who trusted me."

"What else?"

Delgadito flicked dust from his moccasins and withheld comment. No Apache would ever go on the warpath, would ever go on even a single raid, without an ulterior motive, without the promise of material gain. An Apache lived to acquire plunder, whether horses or women or guns. Any Apache who did otherwise, who risked being killed for the mere sake of killing, was regarded as a fool.

"What else?" Cuchillo Negro repeated.

"The whites have many guns, many horses. I would have some of them for my own."

Fiero was frowning. "But why with this white pup you insist on dragging everywhere we go?"

"Who better knows the ways of the whites than another white? Who knows more about their weaknesses and how we can take advantage of those weaknesses? Are not the Apaches who scout for the Army those who cause us the most trouble because they think as we do and can follow us wherever we go?"

"To go with White Apache as an equal is one thing, to let him lead you another," Cuchillo Negro said. "It is not dignified to do such a thing."

"Why? Because of the color of his skin? Can he not hate his kind as much as we do? He saved my life once when he could have left me to die, so I trust his word as I would the word of any of you. I believe him when he says he wants to wage war on his own kind, and I will do as he says until he shows he is not reliable. Should that happen, I will slit his throat and go my own way."

Amarillo was staring at Clay Taggart. "Many guns and horses, you say? How many?"

"More than you can imagine. More than we have stolen from the Mexicans in all the winters we have been raiding them."

Ponce was warming up to the idea too. "If we all did that well, we could have as many wives as we wished. Our people would look up to us. We would not be outcasts."

"We would erase the shame of being caught by Blue Cap," Cuchillo Negro said, betraying his excitement at the prospect.

Disgust and agreement were in harsh conflict on Fiero's features. "All this is well enough, but to let a white man be our leader is more than I can bear."

"You do not need to come," Delgadito said pleasantly. "We will not hold bad feelings if you want to stay and live on the reservation. Look at how many of our brothers have already become farmers. They will welcome you gladly and teach you all you need to know about digging in the dirt with the white man's tools."

"I would rather drink horse urine."

Delgadito stretched and scratched his groin to give Fiero time to ponder the limited choices available. "Maybe you can find some on the reservation who will follow you into Mexico," he suggested. "Maybe you will have better luck avoiding Blue Cap and the other bands of scalp hunters than I did."

"No one would go with me," Fiero said. Temperamental he might well be, but he was also a realist, and he knew that unless he proved himself in a series of successful raids he would never be able to achieve his heart's desire. And here the opportunity was being offered to him—provided he could swallow his pride and accept the leadership of the white cur.

Cuchillo Negro took a half step forward. "I would like to join you, Delgadito."

"You agree to follow White Apache and to do as he says?"

"If you can do it, I can."

Delgadito looked at Amarillo. "And you?"

"I agree."

"And you, Ponce?"

"So long as we get the many horses and guns you have promised, I will let this White Apache direct my steps."

"He will be happy to hear it," Delgadito said, pushing upright. "I must tell him."

"Let him know I will come also," Fiero said.

"You?"

"Why not me?"

"You cannot bear the thought of being led by a white. You just said so."

"I can try."

"Trying is not good enough. You must give your word in advance."

"Since when do Apaches make promises to whites?"

"We must promise him or he will have no reason to believe we are sincere."

"You ask too much."

"Then go your own way. We wish you well," Delgadito said, moving off.

"Wait," Fiero said. He walked over, declaring, "He will need me and you know it. Who else is better than I am at stealing without being caught? Who is better at handling horses? At the silent stalk? With me along you will carry off more plunder than you can hold."

"First you must promise to do as he directs us."

"A white ordering Apaches!" Fiero said indignantly, but when Delgadito started to leave, he hastily added, "Very well. I will do as you wish."

"You must do as *he* wishes."

Fiero's next words were barely audible. "I agree."

"What was that?"

"I said I agree," Fiero rasped. "I will lick this white bastard's feet." His hand touched his knife. "But I warn you. At the first hint of treachery, I'll kill him.

If he proves himself a fool, I'll kill him. And if any of us die because of him, my knife will drink his blood."

"Only if my knife does not drink his blood first."

Clay Taggart was examining newly formed calluses on the soles of his feet when Delgadito sat down beside him. Clay glanced up and asked, "Well, what was the verdict? Did they tell you to go chase your shadow?"

Delgadito had to sort out the possible meaning of the statements before he answered. The word "verdict" was one with which he was unfamiliar, but he didn't bother to ask to have it explained. There was a more pressing matter to resolve first. "We help you," he announced.

"They actually went along with your scheme?" Clay said in disbelief. He looked at the four warriors, and was disturbed to see all four staring at him with what could only be described as quizzical hostility. "I figured they'd rather curl me up and take my hair. Why would they agree to help me?"

"We help you, we help us."

"In what way?"

"We get guns."

Clay pursed his lips. He'd been so elated by the idea of having the Apaches lend a hand that he hadn't given any consideration to the consequences. The Apaches would expect spoils from the raids, especially guns. Guns they'd then use on other whites, innocents who had no connection to his personal vendetta against Miles Gillett.

Delgadito was studying the rancher closely. One thing he had learned during their short time together was that Clay Taggart wore his emotions on his face. Often it was possible for Delgadito to figure out what the white man was thinking just by watching his face. So when he saw Taggart's troubled expression, he mentioned, "We need guns to kill Blue Cap."

"Who?"

"Blue Cap. The one who killed our people."

Clay put two and two together. "Ben Johnson, the scalp hunter. I can't blame you there. You must want revenge on him as bad as I do on Gillett."

"Ben-john-son?" Delgadito said, breaking the name down Apache-style.

"Ben Johnson," Clay repeated. "That's the name of the son of a bitch who slaughtered your band. He deserted the Union cause years ago and has been on the run ever since, making his living by killing and robbing and now lifting scalps."

Delgadito filed the name in his mind. It was one he never wanted to forget. "You see why we need guns?"

"You'll need more than Colts and Winchesters if you're fixing on going after that polecat. His men are as tough as they come, and half of them are breeds. They can track as good as you can, and they fight like wildcats. You'll need a heap of luck to bed them down."

"Bed them down?"

"Kill them. Wipe them out."

Delgadito grunted. "You still like us help?"

"I reckon I can't hold wanting guns against you. Yep, I like the notion just fine."

"There is . . ." Delgadito said, and paused as he tried to find the right word. "Problem," he finished.

"Let me guess. They don't want me carrying a weapon? They want me to do all the squaw work and let them do all the fighting?"

"They want you lead."

"I don't savvy," Clay said, certain the warrior didn't mean what he thought the warrior meant. "Lead what? Any horses we take?"

"Lead us."

A fluttering feather would have floored Clay Taggart. "You want me to lead the war party?"

"Yes?"

"Me?"

"You not want?"

Again Clay looked at the four other Apaches. "They'll let a white man lead them?"

"Yes."

"But why? It makes no sense."

"You know white-eyes better, you speak tongue better. You know where we go, we not been there. You want kill men who hang you, so you pick how they die," Delgadito said. "We do as you want. That all right?"

"I'll be damned," Clay said softly. Who had ever heard of such a thing? He imagined what it would be like to have five fearless, savage Apaches at his beck and call, to have his own small private army, as it were, skilled killers who would dispense justice the way he wanted it done. A new feeling coursed through him, a fleeting feeling of intoxicating power, and he laughed aloud.

"You like?" Delgadito asked.

"I like a lot," Clay admitted, and clapped the Apache on the arm. "You've got yourself a deal, partner. Gillett and his no-account vigilantes will be sorry they ever took the law into their own hands!"

So tickled was Clay Taggart by this unexpected development that he didn't pay much attention to Delgadito. If he had, he might have noticed that the wily Apache was equally jubilant, but for reasons that would have made Clay's skin crawl had he known them. "In eight sleeps we go," he declared. "In eight sleeps killing begin."

"I can hardly wait."

Chapter Nine

Nine days later a war party of six left the Chiricahua sanctuary and trekked stealthily westward. Unlike any other war party ever known, this one included a white man. To make it even more unique, the white man was the actual leader of the war party, a leader who kept wanting to pinch himself to see if he was perhaps dreaming.

Clay Taggart often chuckled when he thought about the nasty surprise in store for those who had hunted him down and hung him. He looked forward with relish to seeing the faces of Jacoby, Hesket, and the rest when the Apaches did their dirty work. Revenge was sweet, but his revenge would be even sweeter because no one would later be able to pin the deaths on him. The Apaches were ideal scapegoats, and the irony was that one of them had come up with the idea. Everything had worked out better than Clay had dared hope it would.

Trotting in the wake of the five warriors, Clay squirmed his toes in the moccasins Delgadito had made for him. Crudely sewn together from a deer hide, they nonetheless protected his feet from prickly cactus and sharp stones. Rising as they did to his knees, they were better protection than his boots would have been and a sight more comfortable.

Clay had had plenty of practice running in them since he hadn't spent the last eight days idle. On the contrary, he had been taken under Delgadito's wing and taught various Apache tricks for living off the land. He'd learned that alamo trees were always a sure sign water was nearby since such trees always grew near water. He was taught which wild berries were edible and which were poisonous. Delgadito showed him how to find certain small roots about the size of gooseberries that tasted delicious raw, much like raw sweet potatoes. And he was treated to sunflower seeds, the first he had ever eaten.

In addition to learning survival, Clay honed his body much as a man honed a knife. Delgadito took him on long runs over the most rugged terrain. He spent hours climbing steep rock walls and trees. And Delgadito gave him lessons in how to blend himself into the background, how to so closely imitate the shape of trees and boulders as to appear like either from a distance.

In exchange, Clay taught the warrior more English. Delgadito was a slow but persistent learner who grew extremely upset at his own mistakes and worked hard to correct them. Clay had no idea why the Apache was so eager to learn the white man's tongue, and he didn't bother to ask.

While all this was going on, the other warriors kept their distance. They would answer Clay when addressed, but otherwise held their peace whenever he was around. He knew they didn't like him, and he didn't really care. So long as he was under Delgadito's watch and care, he was safe. And so long as the Apaches did as he bid, he didn't give a damn how they regarded him.

While on the go, little was said. Clay learned that Apaches rarely talked in the field, except after making camp. They simply ran tirelessly on toward their destination, their bronzed bodies hardly working up a sweat. He surprised himself by being able to keep up, although he suspected Delgadito was setting a slower pace than Apaches normally used.

There was another argument between Delgadito and Fiero the night before the war party left. Not until the second day after leaving Warm Springs did Clay learn the cause. It had something to do with the death of another Apache named El Chico, who'd been killed by Ben Johnson. Apparently Delgadito had implied that El Chico would not have died if Fiero had not been careless, and naturally Fiero had bristled at the accusation.

Of all the Apaches, Clay distrusted Fiero the most. He often caught the warrior giving him looks of sheer hatred, and he had no illusions about what would happen to him should Delgadito die. But he did have an ace up his sleeve. Literally.

The day before they left the refuge, Delgadito had taken Clay aside, reached under his breechcloth, and produced a derringer. "For you."

"You're giving me a gun?" Clay responded, and then wanted to bite his tongue for being so stupid. He quickly took the derringer before Delgadito could change his mind.

"You hide. Savvy?"

"I shouldn't let the others know I have it?"

"No."

"Then I won't."

It comforted Clay to feel the derringer rubbing against his leg as he ran, and he looked forward to soon having a pistol or a rifle. The gift had further confirmed his belief that Delgadito considered him a friend. He'd heard stories of Apaches who occasionally took a liking to white men and befriended them, and he assumed this was another such instance.

At first all went well. They traveled only at night and holed up during the day. At Dragoon Springs they ate an antelope Ponce killed. From there they made their way to the San Pedro River. Twilight was falling when the river came into view, and so did a campfire.

Delgadito called a halt. Turning to Clay, he said, "One should go for look."

Clay stared at Fiero. "You go," he said in his heavily accented Apache. "Tell us what you see."

Lightning leaped from Fiero's dark eyes, but he obeyed without objecting and was soon lost in the gathering darkness.

"I keep expecting him to tear into me," Clay commented in English.

"Him good fighter, good warrior. But never turn back to him," Delgadito cautioned.

"Don't worry. I'm not looking to die."

The Apaches squatted to await their companion, so Clay did likewise. Rather unconsciously he had been adopting many of their mannerisms, and had even gone so far as to tie a wide strip of buckskin around his head to keep his hair in place. He adjusted it as he waited, then folded his arms on his knees.

They didn't have to squat there for long. Within five minutes Fiero was back, reporting to Delgadito, who promptly turned and pointed at Clay. Frowning, Fiero said, "White Apache, there are four Mexicans with four horses and six mules. I saw many packs near their fire. They each have one rifle, one pistol, and one knife."

"We must wait until they sleep, then strike," Amarillo said.

"It has been too long since we ate horseflesh," Ponce added.

Delgadito made a sharp gesture. "The decision is not ours to make. White Apache will decide."

"But they have guns and horses," Ponce protested.

"You promised you would do as he says. You all promised," Delgadito said, gazing at them each in turn.

"We promised to let him lead us in a raid on whites," Fiero mentioned. "Nothing was said about Mexicans."

"This is his raid," Delgadito insisted.

Clay understood enough of the conversation to get the general drift. He stepped forward and stated, "I decide. I, White Apache. And I say no."

Fiero muttered under his breath.

"Why?" Cuchillo Negro asked. Of them all, only he suspected the true motive behind Delgadito's strange pact with the white-eye, and because he did he wasn't as resentful of the rancher's presence. Next to Delgadito, he treated Clay the kindest.

"Must leave no sign," Clay said, struggling for the words. "Must not . . ." He stopped, his limited Apache vocabulary failing him. In English he told Delgadito, "Translate for me. Tell them we can't arouse suspicion by killing these Mexicans. If the Army gets wind of Apaches in this area, they'll have patrols crisscrossing every square mile looking for us. We need to be patient. In another day we'll be at Art Jacoby's ranch and there will be plenty of guns and horses for everyone."

The information was relayed and sullenly accepted. At a word from Clay, Delgadito led them to the northeast, skirting the Mexican camp. They crossed the San Pedro without mishap and struck a northwesterly course.

Clay had previously told Delgadito the general location of the Jacoby ranch. As the farthest removed from Tucson, it was the best choice to be raided first. Jacoby owned several thousand acres nestled in a spacious valley. He raised horses and cattle, the spread boasting about ten seasoned hands who were loyal to the brand and would have to be dealt with if they got in the way.

The remote location of the ranch was only one reason Clay picked it for the raid. Jacoby was a widower and had no children. As much as Clay craved vengeance, he couldn't quite bring himself to unleash the Apaches on a ranch where unsuspecting women and children would be slain. He would have to, eventually, because some of the other posse members did have families. But for now, he could breath a bit easier.

It was close to midnight the next night when the war party crested a low hill and saw in the distance the dark outline of several buildings. Below them were cattle, some of the animals grazing, others sleeping.

"Jacoby?" Delgadito asked.

"This is his spread," Clay verified. He had been here more times than he could count, back in the days when he thought Jacoby was his friend. The layout was as plain as if it was broad daylight. In the middle of the valley stood the modest ranch house, a stable, and a bunkhouse for the hands. A few trees afforded shade on hot days. Otherwise the ground was open. Jacoby hadn't bothered with the upkeep of the shrubs and flowers his wife had so lovingly tended, and they had all died.

"You leader, White Apache," Delgadito said in English. "What you have us do?"

To think about going on a raid was one thing, to be on one and have to decide how to proceed quite another, as Clay now found out. This was all new to him. Should they go after Jacoby first? he asked himself. Or drive off the hands and then kill Jacoby? No, he had a better idea, one that would prevent pursuit. "First off, we take their horses. There's a corral to the south of the stable, and there will be stock in both. We can't make any noise or the ranch hands will be on us with guns blazing."

Delgadito imparted this to the rest.

"Follow me," Clay said, "and stay low." Bending down, he descended the hill and cut across the pasture, always staying far enough from the scattered clusters of cattle to keep them from becoming alarmed. The wind helped since it was blowing in their faces and not the other way around.

Clay felt his stomach muscles bunching tighter and tighter the closer he drew to the buildings. His nerves were as taut as barbed wire, and when a hand fell on his shoulder, he involuntarily jumped.

"There," Delgadito whispered, extending a finger.

A faint glow showed in a bunkhouse window. Clay watched and decided it was a candle, not a lantern, although why the hands should have a candle lit at such a late hour puzzled him. They should all be asleep. He padded on, his hand hovering near the derringer.

The horses in the corral were dozing. Several lifted their heads and snorted as the Apaches came up to the rails. One, a magnificent zebra dun, pranced and nickered, its tail flicking. When Amarillo spoke softly to the animal in Apache, the dun backed away, head bobbing, front hoofs pounding. These were animals accustomed to the scent and sounds of whites, not Indians.

Clay realized as much and rose. "It's all right, big fella," he whispered. "No one is going to hurt you. Calm down."

Ears pricked, the zebra dun quieted somewhat.

"Come on over here," Clay coaxed. "Come on." He beckoned, but the dun refused to come nearer.

Delgadito and Cuchillo Negro moved to the gate, which they opened silently. Each picked a docile animal and swung up using the animal's mane. Hunching low, they goaded their mounts along the rails, forcing the rest of the horses toward the center of the corral. Only the dun gave them trouble.

Dreading discovery, Clay gazed at the bunkhouse. The light in the window had not moved, nor was there any sign the hands had heard the commotion. But if the dun kept acting up, they surely would. Bending, he eased between two rails and walked slowly toward the agitated animal. "It's all right. I'm your friend. How would you like to be scratched between your ears? Or maybe have your neck rubbed?" In this vein he rambled on until he was close enough to reach out and touch the dun. The horse flinched, then fell quiet as he stroked under its chin.

By now Ponce, Amarillo, and Fiero had also picked horses. In unison the Apaches began driving the stock out the gate, each warrior spaced an equal distance from the other. So coordinated were the braves that not a single horse was able to break loose from their cordon.

Only Clay and the zebra dun remained. Stepping next to its shoulder, he hooked his fingers in the thick mane, coiled his legs, and mounted. The dun immediately trotted to the gate and took off after the rest. Clay guided the dun with his knees and his hands while keeping an eye on the building. Amazingly, there was no outcry.

Two hundred yards from the corral, the Apaches halted. Clay caught up, slid down, and motioned at Amarillo. "You watch," he said in Apache. "Stay."

The horses in the stable were next, a half-dozen fine stallions and mares in wide stalls, the best of Jacoby's horses. One of the mares had recently given birth.

Ghosts would have made more noise than the Apaches did as they flitted from stall to stall and led the animals out. This time none of the horses acted up. Presently every last horse on the spread was gathered in a small herd out on the south pasture.

"What next?" Delgadito asked.

Clay pondered a bit. Jacoby was the one he wanted, so he'd spare the hands if he could. They were hardworking cowboys who had done him no wrong. He thought back to his previous visits, and the card games he had taken part in. If he remembered correctly, Jacoby had a gun cabinet in the living room. "We need guns and I know right where to find them."

The Apaches strung out behind Clay as he headed for the rear of the ranch house. At the southeast corner was the back door, which opened onto the kitchen. Clay tested the latch. It moved easily and he slowly pushed the door inward. The hinges gave a single low creak. From within wafted the lingering odors of Jacoby's supper, steak and potatoes.

Clay had been nervous earlier, but it was nothing compared to how he felt now. He was as high-strung as the zebra dun. Every foot was placed down carefully. He probed every shadow. The kitchen table appeared in front of him, so he moved to the right. A chair blocked his way, and he did the same.

At the door to the hall Clay paused to glance back. There were the four Apaches, as motionless as carved wooden figures. He gently pushed on the door and peered into the narrow hallway. Down at the far end was the bedroom where Jacoby slept. The living room was 15 feet away, on the left.

On tiptoe Clay moved along the wall. The house was so quiet that he could hear the grandfather clock in the bedroom ticking even though the door was closed. He entered the living room and strode to the wooden cabinet. A tug on the handle made him want to curse. The twin doors were locked!

Clay tried to remember if Jacoby always locked the cabinet, and had to admit he didn't really know. Nor did he know where the key was kept. Feeling along the top of the cabinet turned up nothing so he turned and crept down the hall to the bedroom door. The Apaches stayed on his heels.

Cautiously Clay opened the door. There was a faint click and he froze. Other than the ticking of the clock, he heard only heavy breathing. Peeking within, he saw Artemis Aaron Jacoby sound asleep, and he was slipping into the room when an object brushed his hand. It was a knife, being offered by Delgadito.

Clay took the Bowie and stepped to the edge of the big bed. Leaning forward, he lightly touched the tip of the blade to Jacoby's throat while whispering, "Rise and shine, you varmint! You've got company calling."

Jacoby's eyes snapped wide in fright, and he might have called out had not Clay's hand clamped on his opening mouth.

"Not a word!" Clay hissed. At a nod from him, Delgadito and Cuchillo Negro came over to seize hold of one of Jacoby's arms. The petrified rancher was hauled roughly erect. "These are my friends,"

Clay said. "One word from me and they'll skin you alive."

"Who—?" Jacoby blurted.

"You mean to say you don't recognize me, pard?"

Jacoby's eyes narrowed, then he gasped and blanched. "Good God!" he cried. "Taggart!"

Clay applied the knife again. "Another shout like that and I'll bury this in you!"

"It can't be! You're dead!"

"You wish I was."

"But your skin, your clothes, your hair! Lord, what's happened to you? Have you gone Indian?"

"It seems to me you should be more interested in what I aim to do to you than what I've been up to since you so kindly made sure that noose was nice and tight."

Jacoby gulped. "I was doing you a favor."

"Like hell you were."

"I was," Jacoby insisted, his voice quavering. "I didn't want them botching the job and have you strangle to death."

"How thoughtful of you," Clay said, gouging the Bowie a little deeper. For the first time since the hanging he let the terrible, all too vivid images flick through his mind. Again he experienced that awful moment of stark panic when the bay shot out from under him. Again he could feel the rope biting into his throat and cutting off his wind. With a supreme effort he checked a shudder and realized Jacoby was speaking.

"Besides, what else could I do? Crane showed up with eight others and deputized me for his posse. I tried to refuse but he told me Gillett had insisted I be on it. The same with Hesket and some of the others."

"I wonder why," Clay said, genuinely curious.

"You know how Crane is. I didn't want to buck him. And after he told me what you'd done . . ."

"What did he say?" Clay snapped. "What lies did he tell you?"

"How was I to know if they were lies or not?"

"*What*, damn you?"

"Crane said that you killed one of Gillett's riders, Vern Boorman. Shot him in the back."

"And you took his word for it? Knowing me as you did? And knowing that Boorman was a hired gun, nothing more?"

"He said there was a witness."

"The mangy liar."

"Mrs. Gillett."

At the mention of the woman he loved, Clay grabbed the front of Jacoby's nightshirt and drew his knife arm back. "What did that son of a bitch say about her? The truth!"

"According to Crane, you tried to force yourself on Mrs. Gillett and Boorman heard her yelling for help and came running. You hid behind a tree and shot Boorman from behind."

So potent was Clay's rage that he could hardly see straight. His vision spinning, his blood pounding in his veins, he shook his head in disgust and said, "If it's the last thing I ever do, Gillett and Crane will pay."

"But why me?" Jacoby asked, practically whining. "You can't blame me for doing as the law wanted."

"Yes, I can. And do you know why? Because you were my friend. You should have done right by me, not turned yellow just because it was Miles Gillett calling the shots."

"You know how powerful he is. Brace him and he plants you. It's as simple as that."

"I would never have turned on *you*."

"Clay, for God's sake! I don't want to die."

The plea fanned a tiny flame of compassion still burning in Clay's breast and he hesitated, unsure of himself and his purpose. Repaying Gillett was all well and good since Gillett was the man responsible for his hanging. The rest, though, were underlings or dupes like Jacoby who didn't have the sand it would take to fill an hourglass. Was it right for him to hold them to account too? Or was he taking his revenge a mite too far?

Jacoby sensed the weakening in the other man's resolve and hastily said, "I know I did wrong, and if I had it to do over again I'd tell Crane to go kiss a mule's butt. I just didn't have time to think it out, is all. One minute I was sitting at the table eating breakfast, the next Crane was pounding on the front door demanding I saddle up and ride with him."

Clay recalled how intimidating Marshal Tom Crane could be, and his knife arm dropped. He glanced at Delgadito, saw the warrior fidget. The Apaches were becoming impatient with him. He had to make up his mind and do it quickly.

"Please, Clay. I can imagine how you must be feeling, but this isn't the answer. Call your friends off and let's sit down over a cup of coffee and talk this out."

"You hung me, damn it," Clay said softly.

"I didn't want to."

Clay weakened, his arm dropping to his side. He avoided looking at Delgadito and tried to think of a way to talk the Apaches into leaving without harming Jacoby.

"Why do you hang your head?" the warrior asked in his own tongue. "Do you no longer want revenge?"

Before Clay could answer, a hand touched his elbow. He turned to find Ponce beside him.

"We need guns, need guns now."

"Why? What is wrong?"

Ponce indicated the window. "Men come."

Chapter Ten

Two lanky cowboys were hurrying toward the ranch house from the bunkhouse. One had his shirt hanging out, the other had on just his socks. Both, though, wore gunbelts.

The White Apache took one look, muttered "Damn!" and strode over to Jacoby. "The key to your gun cabinet. I want it."

Confident that Clay wouldn't hurt him, Jacoby responded arrogantly, "What for? So you can arm these red devils? Not on your life!"

The Bowie seemed to leap up and press against Jacoby's throat of its own accord. "These Apaches did me a favor coming here with me and I don't aim to stand by and let them be wiped out. Give us your guns and we'll go without harming anyone. You have my word."

It was then that Art Jacoby made a mistake that would prove costly not only for him but for all of Arizona. "Your word isn't worth a hell of a lot, old

126

friend. I mean, you claim you're innocent, that you didn't shoot Boorman in the back. But I didn't hear you denying you were with Lilly Gillett. Hell, everyone in these parts knows you're too damn fond of her for your own good. So what if the two of you were in love once? You should have given her up when she wed Gillett and let sleeping dogs lie. But not you. You had to see her on the sly. And now you have the gall to sneak into my house with a pack of murdering Apaches and threaten me at knife point! How the hell do you expect me to trust you?"

Fresh anger welled up in Clay, roiling within him like a thundercloud. He realized that Jacoby had been playing on his sympathy just to weasel out of being killed, that Jacoby never had believed he was innocent, which put Jacoby's role at the hanging in a whole new light. Or rather, the same light in which Clay had first viewed it. "I don't like being played for a fool," he growled.

"Then you have to quit acting like one—"

Clay hauled off and smashed Jacoby in the mouth with the Bowie hilt. Jacoby's head was rocked backward and blood spurted from his upper lip. "I want the key!" Clay said.

"Go to hell!"

Furious now, Clay dashed to the window and saw the pair of cowboys only 20 yards from the front of the house. "Keep him quiet," he ordered in Apache, then ran down the hall and into the living room. At the front door he pressed an ear to the wood and heard footsteps and voices.

" . . . ain't right. I have this feelin'."

"It's probably that darned book you were readin'. A growed man should know better than to stay up late readin' them penny dreadfuls."

"I heard something, I tell you."

"What? The ranch is as quiet as a graveyard."

Neither hand, obviously, had paid much attention to the corral. Clay glanced at the latch, then at the bolt, which hadn't been thrown. He reached up to do so, but froze when scuffing noises told him the cowboys were right on the other side of the door. They just might hear the bolt being pushed.

"I sure hope you know what you're doin'," one of the hands was saying. "The boss will have a fit if you wake him up for no good reason."

"He will, won't he?"

"Sure as shootin'."

"Maybe we should have a look-see around first."

"Now you're thinkin', boy. There's some hope for you yet."

"Okay, Laredo. Where first? The stable?"

"It's as good a place as any. Me, I just want to get this nonsense over with and crawl back under the covers where I belong."

The voices diminished gradually as the cowboys moved away. Clay slid the bolt home and spun. He was shocked to discover Ponce and Fiero watching him intently. "Stay," he told them, and dashed off.

Jacoby was still in the firm grip of Delgadito and Cuchillo Negro. Clay walked up to the rancher and wagged the Bowie in Jacoby's face. "No more playing around, Art. Where's that key?"

"Up your ass!"

Clay cut him. Not deeply, just a swift slash of the razor-sharp blade that split Jacoby's left cheek and elicited a loud gasp. "The next time it's your nose."

"You have gone Indian!" Jacoby declared, terror creeping back into his voice. "You're plumb loco!"

"The *key!*" Clay demanded, wrapping his fingers around his former friend's throat and raising the Bowie to within an inch of Jacoby's nostrils. "I won't ask again."

• Fear made Jacoby tremble. He tried to put on a show of bravery by straightening and squaring his shoulders. "If you think you can make me talk, you're mistaken. You'll never find it." His gaze shifted for a second and he licked his lips.

Clay looked in the same direction. There was a nightstand near the head of the bed, a nightstand with a single drawer. Quickly he crossed over and gave the drawer handle a yank. Inside lay a pistol, a wallet, and several keys. Only one was small, the exact kind that might open the gun cabinet. He plucked it out, then wedged the pistol under the top of his breechclout.

Delgadito saw the gun but made no comment.

"Bring him," Clay directed, hastening to the front room. Fiero and Ponce were at different windows.

"Men are out there," Ponce reported.

"Many men," Fiero said.

The two cowboys had discovered the missing stock and informed the other hands, Clay reasoned, and soon someone would show up at the ranch house to awaken Jacoby. Eagerly he inserted the key, or tried to, but he was holding it upside down. Reversing his grip, he unlocked the right-hand door and swung it open. Ten rifles were lined up neatly in a rack. Boxes of ammunition were stacked underneath the rifles, while to one side, hanging on pegs, were four pistols, two of them ivory-handled. Clay grabbed the two expensive Colts and twirled them on his fingers. "I didn't know you fancied yourself as Wild Bill Hickok," he remarked.

"They were a gift from my brother," Jacoby said sullenly.

"I'll have to send him a note thanking him," Clay said. Turning to Cuchillo Negro, who was the only warrior other than Delgadito that he thought was halfway reliable, he grabbed a third pistol from the nightstand and said, "Here. For you." With that, he gave the gun a toss.

Cuchillo Negro had to let go of Art Jacoby and take a step in order to reach for the spinning revolver. The moment he did, Jacoby twisted and landed a solid right on Delgadito's jaw, staggering the Apache enough so Jacoby could tear his other arm free and dive for the pistol. Desperation lent speed to his limbs. With an inarticulate cry he shouldered Cuchillo Negro aside, caught the pistol on the fly, and swung toward the gun cabinet.

Clay had both of the ivory-handled pistols in his left hand. He saw Jacoby turning toward him, saw Jacoby slipping a finger through the trigger guard. Instantly he flipped one of the ivory-handled pistols into his right hand in the equivalent of a border shift, a difficult stunt requiring much practice. More by luck than design he caught the pistol and cocked both simultaneously just as Jacoby did the same. All three guns thundered at once.

Jacoby's shot was a shade wide. Clay's slugs ripped into the rancher and staggered him rearward. Jacoby tried to steady his aim, but Clay had no intention of giving him the chance. The ivory-handled Colts banged again, and this time Art Jacoby was flung into a rocking chair and crashed to the floor with his arms out flung.

Shouts erupted outside. The high heels of cowboy boots pounded on the earth.

"Get guns!" Clay shouted in Apache. He ran to the nearest window. Shadowy shapes were converging from several directions, and some were almost to the door. There was no use in trying to talk his way out of the fix he was in; Jacoby's hands wouldn't listen to a word he said. They'd want what he wanted, namely revenge, revenge for the slaying of their employer.

All four Apaches were at the gun cabinet. Each had a rifle and was loading it.

Clay had to buy them a little time. Consequently, he fired twice from the hip, aiming high. The bullets shattered the glass panes once kept spotlessly clean by Mrs. Jacoby. Out in the yard the onrushing figures went to ground. As they did, Clay threw himself to the right.

Pistols thundered in an uneven chorus. Slugs punched into the windowsill, the jambs, and the wall. Some zinged across the room, shattering a lamp and a vase. There were more shouts.

The Apaches had dropped low at the first volley and were heading for the hall. Clay raced after them. Delgadito paused to offer him a Winchester.

"Here. It is loaded."

Clay already had the derringer and the Bowie slanted under his breechcloth. Now he added the two Colts. There was a loud thump against the front door, as if someone had rammed it with a shoulder, followed by an earsplitting crash as the door buckled inward. Clay whirled, saw two figures framed in the doorway, and dived flat. Pistols cracked, spitting death, and slugs tore into the wall above him, sending wood chips flying. Clay had no choice but to fire, the Winchester bucking against his shoulder. One of the figures dropped. The other retreated out of sight.

Pushing upright, Clay sprinted down the hall to the kitchen. Ponce was just opening the rear door, but as he did a volley blasted the upper panel to splinters. Clay and the four Apaches crouched down while the hail of lethal lead poured into the house from front and back.

Clay's mind was racing. The cowboys had them pinned down front and back, effectively trapped. Or were they? No shots sounded on either side of the house, which meant there were avenues of escape if they were daring enough to try. "Come!" he called out, rotating on a heel.

The door to the drawing room where Mrs. Jacoby had once played the piano and knitted was wide open. Clay sped to the window, squatted, and raised his eyes to the sill. There was a single tree partway between the house and the stable but no indication of movement. Gripping the sash, he lifted the window high. A puff of wind fluttered the curtains. Clay gestured at the warriors, then swiftly eased over the sill and checked in both directions before darting toward the tree.

Both in front and behind the ranch house the firing had tapered off. Clay came to the tree and crouched at its base. There were five or six cowboys edging toward the front doorway and another two visible at the back. Clay was about to rise and run to the corral when a hand circled his ankle. It was Delgadito, lying flat. So were the other Apaches.

Clay did as they were doing. Lizard-like, the warriors scuttled into the open, their bodies so low to the ground that they appeared part of it. Half-expecting to get a bullet in the back, Clay crawled awkwardly forward, the Winchester in his left hand. They were nearly to the corral when enraged yells signaled the discovery of Jacoby's body.

Clay let the Apaches lead him from there on out. They knew exactly what to do, and did it with such skill that had he not been right there with them he would never have believed they were there. Soundlessly they snaked under the bottom rail, crossed the corral, and snaked out the far side. There Delgadito angled into the foot-high grass.

A flurry of activity was taking place at the ranch house. Cowboys were running back and forth, calling to one another as they sought the war party. As yet none had come anywhere near the corral or the stable.

Clay, the last to enter the pasture, smiled at the outcome of the raid. He'd settled accounts with Jacoby, the first of those who were going to pay for the outrage against him, and settled too his determination to repay each and every one of them in kind. He'd let Jacoby get to him, let himself have second thoughts. That would never happen again.

The commotion at the ranch was spreading as the hands fanned out. Since all the horses were gone, they had to search on foot. Many were cursing or boasting of what they would do when they caught the Indians.

There was a time when Clay Taggart would have considered such behavior to be perfectly normal. Had his own spread been attacked, his three hands would no doubt have done the same. But now, judging the cowboys by Apache standards, he regarded the hands as noisy jackasses who couldn't find a bull in a barnyard. Small wonder that Apache raids were usually successful when their enemies advertised their every move and made ideal targets.

About 50 of the 200 yards to where Amarillo waited with the stolen stock had been covered when Clay became aware of cowboys in the pasture. Slowing, he glanced over his shoulder and distinguished the inky silhouettes of four men advancing in a row.

The Apaches quickened their pace, so Clay did the same. Ponce was only a few feet in front of him, yet Clay never heard so much as the rustle of grass. He tried to be as quiet, but his clumsy efforts were like those of a toddler in comparison to the supple grace of the seasoned warriors.

"Hey! What's that up yonder?" a hand called out.

"Where?" another answered.

Clay tensed and tried to go even faster.

"There! Don't you see 'em?"

Gunfire stabbed the night, four shots so swift they blended into one, the handiwork of a cowboy partial to fanning his Colt instead of squeezing the trigger.

Hornets swarmed past Clay Taggart. His first instinct was to flatten, but then he saw the Apaches rise into crouches and bound off like antelope, so once again he relied on their experience and did exactly as they did. The gunfire increased as the first cowboy's pards joined in. A bullet nicked Clay's shoulder, stinging only slightly. He heard Ponce grunt.

"They're over here!" a hand was bellowing for the benefit of the cowhands near the stable and the house. "This way! The sons of bitches are gettin' away!"

Clay certainly hoped so. He ran for dear life, his legs a blur. One fact he had definitely learned; it was a hell of a lot easier to run in moccasins than it was in high-heeled boots. Small wonder Apaches were noted for being fleet of foot.

The band swiftly outdistanced the cowboys. A compact mass materialized in the darkness. Then they were at the horses, each Apache vaulting onto the nearest animal. Not so Clay. He searched, saw the zebra dun standing aloof from the others, and sprang to its side. The dun shied, taking a few steps, but soft words from him calmed it and he was able to swing up.

The Apaches spread out around the stolen stock. The warriors at the rear, Amarillo and Fiero, cut loose with earsplitting yips that galvanized the herd into motion to the southwest. Rifle and pistol fire attended their flight, but now the cowboys were shooting at shadows and none of the shots came anywhere close.

Clay had lost sight of Delgadito, and found himself riding close to Fiero, of all people. The warrior
glanced at him, then showed teeth. This was Fiero's
element and he was as happy as could be. Clay
returned the smile, and for a moment the two
of them shared an emotional bond. The moment
passed, however, when Fiero galloped on ahead,
whooping like a madman.

The zebra dun galloped smoothly, its sleek muscles rippling. Clay had often ridden bareback when
younger, but wasn't used to riding without a bridle.
He locked his fingers in the mane and pressed his
knees a bit tighter than he ordinarily would. The
rush of wind felt soothing on his hot face. He hadn't
realized how much he had been sweating until that
moment.

Cattle scattered out of the path of the horses.
Some, startled from sleep, took off as if shot
from cannons; they wouldn't stop until they were
so exhausted they couldn't go another foot.

When the Apaches gained the crest of the low
hill, they slowed the horses to a walk. Clay shifted
to look back. There were lights on in the house,
the bunkhouse, and the stable. He saw no sign of
pursuit and grinned. His idea to take all the horses
before doing anything else had been the right one.

Through the dry Arizona night the war party fled.
Golden streaks heralding the dawn were the signal
to ride deep into the cover of heavy brush. Fiero
and Amarillo tied the horses. Cuchillo Negro trotted
off to check their back trail. Clay, feeling tired but
oddly contented, walked to where Delgadito and
Ponce were showing each other the rifles they had
acquired. He was shocked to see a large red stain on
Ponce's shirt. "You took a slug!" he blurted out in
English, then caught his mistake and said in Apache,
"You were shot."

Ponce gave Clay a quizzical sort of look. "Yes," he answered simply.

"Does it hurt?" Clay asked.

"No more than being ripped open by a mountain lion."

"Let me see."

"Why?"

"You may need . . ." and here Clay paused because he couldn't think of the right word.

Delgadito came to Clay's rescue. "White Apache wants to see if you need mending."

"I will mend myself," Ponce said with a touch of indignation. "Does he think I am a child that I need someone to look after me?"

"I want to help," Clay explained. And he truly did, but for a rather selfish reason that he wouldn't bring himself to admit openly; already he was looking ahead to the next raid, perhaps on Hesket's spread. He'd need all of the Apaches in prime health if he was to pull it off since Hesket would be much harder to get at. Not to mention the chore it would be going after Miles Gillett. So until his vengeance was satisfied, he wanted to keep the Apaches alive.

Ponce was none too pleased, but he reluctantly pulled at his shirt, raising it high enough for the wound to be seen.

Clay gaped. The slug had torn through the warrior from back to front, low down on the right side, and blood flowed from both the entry and exit wounds. The latter was a full inch in diameter, a jagged hole made when the slug blew out a sizeable chunk of flesh. He was amazed the warrior wasn't doubled over in agony. "If that gets infected, he might die," Clay said in English to Delgadito. "What can we do for him?"

"You watch. Learn."

A small fire was made. While Delgadito fanned the flames, Ponce took a .44-40 shell and used a knife to pry at the case head until he separated it from the case. Ponce then poured the powder into his left palm.

Clay watched with interest, unable to figure what use the gunpowder would be until he saw Ponce pour some into both the entry and exit wounds. "You're not . . ." he said in disbelief.

Delgadito was holding the end of a short stick in the fire. Lifting it, he waited a few seconds to be certain the flames flicking at the end of the stick wouldn't go out, then gave the firebrand to the other warrior.

Ponce never hesitated. He sat down, bent a little forward, reached behind him, and applied the brand to the exit wound. The instant the flames touched the gunpowder there was a blinding flash and a loud sizzling, as of meat roasting on a spit. Flame and smoke shot from the bullet hole, both front and back, and the acrid stench of burnt flesh filled the air.

Clay Taggart felt his stomach churn and took a step backward, his hand over his mouth and nose. He had been staring at Ponce's face the whole time and not once had he seen the warrior show any great pain. Ponce had gritted his teeth and arched his back when the gunpowder ignited, but he hadn't cried out.

"Remember," Delgadito told Clay in English. "Maybe one day you do."

"Never," Clay assured him. "It'll be a cold day in hell before I do a harebrained thing like that."

"You do when have to."

"Never," Clay reiterated, and gave a shudder at the mere thought.

Just then Fiero and Amarillo walked up. The former hefted the rifle he had stolen and declared, "Now many white-eyes die! Our medicine is as strong as theirs!"

"Thanks to White Apache," Delgadito said.

Fiero showed his contempt. "Who made so much noise it was a wonder the Americans did not learn we were there sooner, and who spent so much time talking to that other white-eye that we were almost trapped in the wood lodge. White Apache is not much of a leader."

"He will get better," Delgadito stated.

"I will not be there to see it," Fiero said. "I agreed to follow this white pet of yours this one time. I did not agree to follow him always. From this moment on, I make war on my own. I do as I want to do."

"You will miss our next raid, and there will be more horses and guns for everyone who goes."

"When will it be?"

Delgadito swiveled toward Clay. "When?"

"I don't know," Clay confessed in English. The issue of when to strike Hesket was one he hadn't even considered yet. "Don't we have to take care of the stock we have now before we go get more? What are we going to do with all these horses anyway?"

"Feed my people," Delgadito said.

"We're not keeping any for ourselves?" Clay asked, but before he could receive a reply, Cuchillo Negro raced out of the brush.

"Big trouble," he announced. "The *Americano* Army is after us."

Chapter Eleven

The war party dashed to the edge of the brush, Clay Taggart bringing up the rear. From under cover they could clearly see a column of dust far to the northwest and a dozen or more vague figures galloping hard toward them. "How do you know they are Army?" Clay asked in his imperfect Apache.

"Do you not have eyes?" Cuchillo Negro responded.

"I see many dark shapes. Riders too far off to tell who they are."

"Not too far for me, White Apache."

Delgadito agreed with Cuchillo Negro. He too could see the telltale blue of uniforms and the glint of sunlight on buttons and insignia. "It is a patrol," he declared.

Fiero gave a fierce scowl. "Let them come! We will lie in wait and ambush them!"

"We have guns as good as theirs so we have no reason to run," Ponce agreed heartily, his wicked wound forgotten. "Think of how many more horses and weapons will be ours!"

None of the warriors glanced at Clay. If they had, they would have noticed the worry in his eyes. The last thing he wanted to do was engage a cavalry patrol. Killing the men who had strung him up was one thing since they had been vigilantes working outside the law. Killing soldiers would be quite another since they were simply men doing their job. There was no excuse for doing so, not for him, at least. The Apaches had a grievance with the Army. He didn't.

Worse, Clay was afraid of what would happen if some of the soldiers escaped and reported that a white man was riding with a band of Chiricahuas. The word would spread like wildfire and result in his being the most sought-after individual in all of Arizona. Hell, in all of the Southwest. Other whites would judge him a traitor to their kind, and there would be a large bounty put on his head. He couldn't let that happen.

Clay cleared his throat as he tried to sort out the correct words. "I say we ride away. We have many guns, many horses. Not need more."

"You can go if you want," Fiero sneered. "We will stay and show the Americans that we are men of courage."

"And Blue Cap?"

"What about him?" Fiero demanded.

"Who kills him if you die? Who does to him as he did to your band?"

The question brought silence. Delgadito shared Clay's sentiments, but he held his tongue to see whether Clay could hold his own alone.

"We already have plenty horses, plenty guns," Clay continued. "We should go hide in Dragoons. Plan next raid."

"I do not like running away," Fiero said stubbornly.

"Not running," Clay said, wishing he could be more eloquent. His best bet was to use small words, those he knew best. "Save our lives now so we live to hunt down Blue Cap and his men later."

Amarillo joined the conversation. "You will help us kill Blue Cap?"

"The five of you helped me. I can do no less."

Of all the warriors, none was more pleased by this unexpected news than Delgadito. He wanted Taggart to join them when they went after the scalp hunters, and secretly he had been trying to think of a means of persuading the white man to lend a hand. Now Clay was unwittingly playing right along with Delgadito's long-range plans.

Ponce stared at the approaching troopers. "White Apache speaks wise words. Perhaps we should do as he wants. I, for one, want to kill Blue Cap more than I do these soldiers."

"We go then," Delgadito said, turning before Fiero could object. He didn't look back to see if they followed, but counted on his former influence among them to bring them all in line. Despite his many protests to the contrary, he hadn't given up the idea of being a leader among his people again one day. To this end had he taken Clay Taggart under his wing. Taggart was the tool Delgadito would use to achieve his goal, and the beauty of Delgadito's plan was that not once would Taggart ever suspect the role he was playing.

In short order they were mounted and riding to the southeast. Since their animals were extremely tired after the long night spent on the move, they had to goad the horses into a gallop.

Clay tried to guess how the patrol had found their trail so quickly. It was unlikely the alarm had been spread by any of the Bar J hands since they were all afoot and couldn't have reached any of the neighboring ranches so soon. He favored the idea that the patrol had simply stumbled on their tracks and was coming to investigate. Or there could very well be an Apache scout with the patrol, in which case the scout might have read something from the pattern of tracks that told him some of his own people were involved. In any event, Clay knew he was in for a long, hot day.

The prediction proved accurate. For the next three hours the war party fled on across the blistering landscape. By mid-morning the temperature was in the nineties and still climbing. Sweat poured from Clay's body, but the Apaches, as usual, were hardly bothered by the heat. The horses, though, shared Clay's distress, and Clay began to think they'd end up riding the poor animals into the ground if they weren't more careful.

At last, to Clay's relief, Delgadito led them to a spring situated below a barren rise. Cuchillo Negro climbed to the top, and returned to report that the cavalry patrol was still after them and had gained considerable ground. The news spurred the Apaches to hurry the horses on.

Clay would have liked to rest a while. His backside was sore, as were his thighs, a consequence of not having done any riding since his hanging. He closed his mind to the discomfort, ignoring it as he would an annoying fly, and kept on going.

Another hour elapsed. Delgadito glanced around, saw the dust cloud less than half a mile off, and slowed the horses to a walk. At a gesture from him, the rest of the warriors converged, except for Ponce, who stayed at the rear to keep any of the stock from straying. "The Americans must be delayed," Delgadito informed them. "One of us must ride back and slow them down."

"I will go," Fiero offered.

"And I," Cuchillo Negro volunteered.

"No, let it be me," Ponce said.

Delgadito looked at Clay and reverted to English. "You are one should pick. You are leader on this raid."

"Not by choice," Clay grumbled. "Choose whichever one you want. It makes no difference to me."

"Ponce hurt. He should not go."

"Then let it be Cuchillo Negro."

"Not good. I go. *Shee-dah.*"

"Why you?"

"I know when leave. Others maybe get killed."

Clay was impressed by Delgadito's concern for the others, but he was loathe to let his only friend among the band go off to possibly be slain. Where would that leave him? he reflected. There was little doubt that either Fiero or Ponce would kill him the first chance they got. "You shouldn't go alone," he cautioned. "Take me with you."

"This not your fight."

"You wouldn't be in this fix if it wasn't for me. I'm going, and that's final."

"If you want," Delgadito said with deceptive innocence. He translated the gist of their talk for the others, then wheeled his mount. A flick of Delgadito's heels and he was racing to intercept the cavalry while behind him pounded the *pindah lickoyee* who was snared in his clever web and didn't even realize it.

Clay Taggart stared at the tall Apache's broad back and longed to be elsewhere as he succumbed to second thoughts about his decision to go along. After all, since he wasn't about to fire on the cavalry no matter what happened, of what use could he be? The temptation to veer off into the brush and keep on going was almost overpowering.

Suddenly Degadito came to a shallow arroyo and reined up in its bed. Vaulting down, he dashed to the west side and went prone, then crawled to the rim and peeked over. The patrol was near enough for him to make out the mustaches many of the whites wore on their upper lips. Hairy caterpillars, his people called them. He worked the lever of his Winchester, feeding a cartridge into the chamber.

Clay was also staring at the patrol, and when he heard the metallic rasp of the warrior's rifle, he wanted to jump up and shout a warning. But he didn't. He was rooted to the ground both by his friendship for Delgadito and his uncertainty over what sort of reception he would get from the soldiers. He still didn't know if Marshal Crane had sent word to the nearest military posts that he was wanted by the law before Crane learned of his whereabouts and came after him with the posse, and he wasn't about to blunder and be tossed into a stockade.

At the forefront of the column rode a swarthy scout, a full-blooded Apache in proper Army uniform whose head was bent so he could read the tracks of the stolen herd. His long black hair hung well past his shoulders, and across his chest was slanted a gleaming cartridge belt.

Delgadito took a bead on the scout. There was no hatred on his countenance, no resentment over a fellow warrior turned traitor. He lightly pressed his finger to the trigger, held his breath to steady his aim, and when the scout was within range, he fired.

The retort rolled out across the flatland bordering the arroyo. Blasted off his horse, the scout toppled. The body had no sooner hit the ground than another shot sounded and a soldier bearing chevrons on his sleeves was hurled from the saddle as if by an unseen fist.

Clay heard the officer in command bellow and watched as the column split down the middle, half going right, half going left. Legs flailing, the soldiers rode madly for the cover of brush over a hundred yards away. Some cut loose with carbines.

Delgadito worked his Winchester calmly, methodically, heedless of the slugs thudding into the earth within feet of his head. He shot a cavalryman on the right, then one on the left. And he would have shot more too had his rifle not been batted aside.

"That's enough!" Clay said. "Let's vamoose."

"We not done."

"They'll lay low for a while before closing in on us," Clay said. "We should hightail it out of here while we still can."

"I stay. You go."

"No, damn it. We both should skedaddle," Clay insisted, partly because he didn't care to see Delgadito gunned down, partly because he didn't want any more of the soldiers to be shot, and partly because he wanted to get the hell out of there before any of the troopers got a good look at him and saw he wasn't an Apache.

"I wait while," Delgadito said, refusing to be hurried.

Galled by the warrior's attitude, Clay hunkered down and scanned the arroyo to the north and the south. Eventually the cavalrymen would get around to working along the bed, and then it would only be a matter of time before he and Delgadito were caught in a cross fire. Couldn't the Apache see that?

An eerie quiet had descended. Not so much as a bird twittered. Clay wiped sweat from his forehead and nervously fingered the trigger guard of his rifle.

Delgadito might as well have been carved from solid rock for all the life he showed. But appearances could be deceiving. Although the Apache faced straight ahead, his eyes repeatedly flicked to both sides and his keen ears were strained to their limit. He knew well before Clay did when men were coming toward them. He even knew how many. And when he judged the timing to be right, he whirled, gave Clay a shove, and said, "Run! They are on us!"

Clay bolted without thinking. He was halfway to the zebra dun when he saw several troopers on foot to the south, at a bend in the arroyo. The foremost trooper had a carbine tucked to a shoulder and was taking aim—*at Clay!* Clay reacted in the only way possible. He shifted, crouched, and snapped off a shot from the waist. To his horror, his slug slammed into the trooper's chest and knocked the man flat.

Carbines spat lead from various points as Clay seized hold of the dun's mane. The frightened horse started to run, and Clay barely jumped on in time. Up and out of the arroyo they swept, bearing eastward. There were angry shouts from the soldiers. Scattered gunfire punctuated the shouts, the gunfire dwindling the further Clay went.

Not until the shooting stopped did Clay check on Delgadito. He smiled on seeing the Apache close behind, and when the warrior smiled back, he took it as yet another sign that Apaches weren't the heartless fiends most whites took them for.

Actually, however, Delgadito's smile had nothing whatsoever to do with friendship. Delgadito was happy because his ploy had worked and he was eager to point out the implications at the first opportunity.

Together they flew along under the glaring Arizona sun, the bronzed brave and the rancher whose own skin was now burned a deep reddish brown. For miles they rode, until, on a hillock, they stopped to give their mounts a breather.

Clay shifted, saw a dust cloud. "They're still after us," he remarked.

"They not give up easy."

"No, I reckon they won't," Clay said absently.

"Not after we kill so many," Delgadito said. Then, to drive home the point he wanted to make, he added, "Not after you kill one." By the darkening of the white man's features, he knew his reminder had the desired effect.

I shot a trooper! Clay thought, aghast. He'd gone and done exactly what he hadn't wanted to do! If somehow word ever reached the Army, his hide wouldn't be worth a plugged nickel anywhere in the whole blamed country. The Army would never stop trying to find him. They might even post a bounty.

Suddenly Miles Gillett seemed the least of Clay's troubles. He wanted to quit the war party, to leave the Apaches and head for parts unknown where he could start over. Taking up a new identity was easy. All he had to do was start calling himself by a new name and a brand-new life was his for the taking.

Then Clay remembered Lilly, and how Miles Gillett had treated the woman he loved. He remembered how Gillett had played him for a fool, and the hanging. A new life would have to wait until accounts were settled or he'd never be able to look himself in the mirror again.

It was early evening when Clay and Delgadito caught up with their band in a gulch shaded by willows.

"The Americans?" Cuchillo Negro asked.

"They still come," Delgadito answered.

"Did you slay any?" Fiero asked hopefully.

"I shot four. White Apache shot one."

Cuchillo Negro gave Clay a clap on the arm. "I need no other proof that you are one of us. Only someone who hates whites as much as we do would

make war on the blue coats. Only someone who is
Apache at heart would do as you have done."

"I did what I had to," Clay mumbled, resisting a
wave of guilt and despair.

"We must kill more if we are to stop them," Fiero
commented.

"No!" Clay blurted out, and five heads swung
toward him. He read suspicion on the faces of three
of them, so he went on hastily. "There is better way.
Why risk our lives?"

"What is this better way?" Ponce asked.

"We take their horses tonight," Clay proposed.
"Leave them on foot."

The Apaches exchanged looks, and it was impossible to tell from their features whether they liked
the idea or not. Clay prayed they would. He'd been
lucky earlier, and had been able to get away without
any of the troopers realizing he was a white man. He
didn't care to push his luck by locking horns with
the patrol again.

Delgadito would rather have slain as many troopers as he could, but he saw the secret fear deep in
Clay Taggart's eyes and he opted not to push the
white man into doing something that would cause
Taggart to rebel, thus spoiling everything. "I will do
as White Apache wants," he announced. "It will be
a fine trick to steal their horses from under their
noses and to let the sun bake their brains as they
walk back to the fort."

All the others agreed, with a single exception.

"We have enough horses now," Fiero said in disgust. "The blood of our people cries out for the blood
of the whites."

"Kill them," Clay said, desperate to convince the
hothead to go along with his idea, "and many more
come. So many maybe we not reach mountains."

"I am not scared of *Americanos*," Fiero boasted.

"Nor are we," Delgadito said. "But it is the way of the Shis-Inday to steal without being caught, to kill without being killed. Would you have us waste our lives when so much remains to be done?"

"No," Fiero said begrudgingly.

"Then we steal their horses," Delgadito said, and only he noticed when the white-eye turned away and sighed in relief.

Darkness descended shortly thereafter. Amarillo climbed a willow and reported, "I see their fire."

"Far?" Clay asked.

"No."

A hurried talk resulted in Ponce being left to watch the stolen horses while the rest crept toward the patrol. In order to have their hands free, the Apaches didn't take their rifles, which weren't needed anyway since every warrior now had a belt gun.

Clay deliberately hung back. The enveloping darkness did little to erase his dread of being caught. If that happened, he'd be sent up before a firing squad. It was as simple as that. Not a single soul in all of Arizona would have any sympathy for a white man dastardly enough to align himself with the scourges of the Southwest.

The officer in charge of the troopers, who obviously knew something of Apache nature, had set up his camp by the book. A small fire had been made at the center, with the mounts tethered close at hand. All the brush within 30 feet of the encampment had been cleared away and sentries posted on two sides. No one could get anywhere near the horses without being spotted. Or so the cavalrymen believed.

From behind a bush 50 yards out, Clay studied the arrangement, and repressed a shudder when he saw five bodies wrapped tight in blankets. If only he could go back and undo what had been done! He was a rancher, not a killer. At least he hadn't had to kill *many* men over the years, and those he had killed had deserved it.

Delgadito turned and whispered, "You stay." At a nod from him, the Apaches melted into the night.

Lying flat, Clay rested his chin on his forearms and pondered his course of action once the band reached the sanctuary of the Dragoons. He intended to persuade the Apaches to raid Bill Hesket's ranch next, or maybe Frank Bitmer's. Gillett would be saved for last, the way dessert was saved for the last part of a meal. Revenge, like dessert, should be savored slowly.

Suddenly a figure appeared between the camp and Clay's position. Silhouetted against the flickering fire was the outline of a stocky form crawling toward the troopers. Clay was shocked that one of the warriors would be so careless, then realized only he could see the brave. The soldiers only saw a black wall beyond the perimeter of their camp.

Clay reached for a pistol, but changed his mind. No matter what happened, he wasn't going to kill another soldier. He'd let them kill him first.

The silhouette disappeared. From the camp came low voices. There was no laughter, no singing. The troopers were too upset over the loss of their comrades to banter back and forth.

Minutes stretched into an hour, an hour into two. Clay dozed despite his best efforts to stay awake. He had been on the go for too long without rest, without food. A strident screech brought him fully awake in an instant, his heart beating madly as he rose on his knees. Whoops and yips rent the air. Startled troopers leaped to their feet, frantically feeding cartridges into their carbines.

The cavalry mounts broke into motion, galloping eastward, at their rear a lone Apache on horseback goading them on. A sentry took aim at the warrior's back, and from the ring of darkness came the blast of pistols, crumpling the trooper before a hail of lead.

Soldiers whirled and began firing wildly despite the shouts of their officer and a sergeant. Most of them were young, inexperienced. Their imaginations got the better of their logic, and they spied Apaches where just shadows existed. Blasting right and left, they peppered the area with gunfire.

Clay Taggart threw himself flat once more as slugs bit into the earth or whizzed overhead. A bullet clipped a branch from the bush and it fell on his head. Scrambling rearward, he sought to put some distance between the troopers and himself. So intent was he on the camp that he didn't realize the cavalry mounts were heading directly toward him until the thunder of their hoofs was too loud to be ignored.

Glancing around, Clay beheld the horses in a tight mass, their manes flying as they fled in a panic. He pushed upright and bolted southward, covering a mere two yards when he tripped and fell. The drumming of shod hoofs was loud in his ears as he shoved erect a second time. A glance showed him the horses were only a dozen feet away. Clay sprinted at his top speed to get out of their path, but his top speed wasn't good enough because a moment later something slammed into his shoulder with the force of a battering ram.

Chapter Twelve

Whether Clay hit his head as he crashed down or whether a flying hoof was to blame, he never knew. Suddenly the world went black. When next Clay opened his eyes, he was amazed to see a ring of dirt streaked faces looming above him, not Apaches either, but the hate-filled faces of a dozen or more troopers. He realized his arms were bound behind his back and he could feel great pressure on his lower legs.

"I say we kill the son of a bitch right here and now," a cavalryman sporting a sweeping mustache suggested.

"Let's start by cutting out the bastard's eyes," proposed another, who instantly produced a glittering knife.

Clay lay helpless as a calloused hand reached for his throat. He was about to blurt out that he was a white man and hopefully forestall being slain when a stern voice stopped the hand in midair.

"That will be quite enough of that, Private Williams. Put the knife away this instant."

Private Williams hesitated, his disappointment obvious. "Please, Captain. This stinking savage and his rotten friends killed Hank and all the others! He deserves a slow, painful death, and we're just the ones to give it to him!"

Some of the others murmured assent, their eyes glittering like barbed arrow tips in the flickering glow from the nearby campfire.

A square-shouldered man wearing chevrons on his sleeves bulled his way between two of the troopers and glared at Williams. "You heard the captain, Private. Do as he tells you and put that toothpick away or you'll be on report when we get back." He leaned forward, his jaw muscles twitching. "Not only that, you'll get me riled, and the last thing you ever want to do is *get me riled*."

The private showed no inclination to argue. "Sorry, Sergeant Conover. I didn't mean no disrespect." The knife promptly disappeared. "It's just that I'm so damn mad I can't think straight."

"It's all right this once, son," Conover said. "We're all mighty high-strung over what's happened. I know this is your first hitch in Arizona and you're not accustomed to all this bloodshed, but you've got to remember that you're a professional soldier, Detachment C, Fifth Cavalry, the pride of the United States Army. You have a job to do and you'll do as you're told."

Another man appeared, a handsome man whose rigid bearing marked him as their officer. He studied Clay carefully and remarked, "If it's any consolation, Private Williams, for two bits I'd skin this son of a bitch myself."

Clay was at a loss to know what to do. Clearly they mistook him for an Apache, thanks to the dim light, his bronzed skin, his breechcloth, and his headband. He could easily convince them otherwise, but what would happen then? Would they be inclined to cut him loose and let him go his own way? Not hardly, not after they'd lost so many of their companions. On the contrary, they just might become so mad that he'd been part of the war party—that a white man would turn traitor and side with the Apaches— they'd kill him then and there, no matter what the officer or sergeant wanted.

"All right, men," the captain said. "Turn in and try to get some rest. We have a long march ahead of us tomorrow and we need to be refreshed."

"But what about those heathen Apaches?" a trooper asked.

It was Sergeant Conover who answered. "They got what they were after, soldier. Our horses."

"Won't they come back and try and save this one?" the same trooper inquired, nudging Clay with his boot.

"You don't know Apaches very well," Sergeant Conover said. "They're not about to lay down their lives for one of their own. They don't have the same kind of loyalties white folks do." He glanced at the prisoner. "As far as they're concerned, this one is paying the price for being stupid enough to be caught. They'd let him rot before they'd lift a finger to help him."

Clay knew the sergeant was wrong, but he couldn't very well set the man straight. He suddenly became aware that the pressure on his legs had lifted and he looked down to see a skinny trooper standing. The man had been sitting on him while tying his ankles tight.

The troopers dispersed by ones and twos. Only the officer, the sergeant, and three others were still there when Conover abruptly leaned down for a closer inspection of Clay and blurted out, "What the hell!"

"What is it, Sergeant," the officer wanted to know.

"I'm not rightly sure, Captain Vance," Sergeant Conover said. He slipped his hands under Clay's shoulders and nodded at a private. "Norris, give me a hand and move this savage closer to the campfire."

Worry gnawed at Clay's innards as he was roughly lifted and dumped so close to the flames they nearly singed his left shoulder. His jaw was gripped by Conover, his face turned toward the fire. Its brightness made him squint.

"I don't believe it!"

"What?" the captain demanded, walking over. "What has you so excited?"

"Look at his eyes, sir," Sergeant Conover said. "Look at this man's eyes!"

Captain Vance bent low and stared at Clay for a full ten seconds. "I'm looking, and I don't see anything out of the . . ." He stopped, his mouth going slack, his own eyes widening in shock. "Jesus!" he declared. "They're blue!"

Clay could see some of the other troopers returning. The word was being whispered about the camp and more were converging. He tensed, expecting the worst, but kept his features calm so they wouldn't suspect how upset he was at their discovery.

"And look at this, sir," Sergeant Conover said, kneeling and touching a hand to Clay's exposed ear. "His hair is much too short for an Apache. Not even the reservation bucks wear it this short, and they're supposed to." Conover ran a palm over Clay's upper arm. "Another thing. His skin is lighter than any Apache I ever saw. If I didn't know better, Captain, I'd swear that this here is a white man."

Murmuring broke out among the troopers. A few fingered their weapons. Not a one showed a hint of friendliness.

Vance sank to one knee and regarded Clay thoughtfully. "I find it too incredible to believe." He paused, then addressed Clay directly. "Do you savvy English, mister? Do you speak the white man's tongue?"

Here was the moment of truth. Clay only had to say a single word. But he hesitated, thinking of the likely outcome if he should have to go up before a military tribunal. The Army had final jurisdiction where renegades were concerned, red or otherwise, and they weren't about to go easy on a man who had killed one of their own. He adopted a blank stare that he hoped would be convincing.

"He doesn't understand you, sir," Sergeant Conover said. *"Habla español, blanco Apache?"*

Although Clay spoke enough Spanish to comprehend, he continued pretending not to understand. He spotted Private Williams and several other men talking excitedly and giving him the sort of looks reserved for condemned killers.

Private Norris cleared his throat. "Maybe he was taken by the Apaches when he was little and raised by them. I hear they do that from time to time."

"If so, it's damn odd we haven't heard something about him before now," Captain Vance said.

"Norris might be on to something, sir," Sergeant Conover said. "This hombre looks about twenty or twenty-five years old to me. If the Apaches got ahold of him that long ago, there wouldn't be a record of it." His brow furrowed. "But that wouldn't explain why his hair is so short and why his skin isn't darker."

Captain Vance clasped his hands behind his back and pondered. "It's a mystery others will have to solve. We'll notify the Indian agent once we're back at the fort and see if he can find out anything."

Private Williams and two others walked up. "Sir, we couldn't help but overhear," Williams said, "and we'd respectfully like to ask that you change your mind."

"Private!" Conover exploded, rising.

"No, Sergeant," the officer said, holding out a restraining hand. "Let him speak his piece. You know that my policy is to always listen to any suggestions my men have to make."

"Thank you, sir," Williams said. He jabbed a finger at Clay. "Now about this prisoner of ours. Whether he's white or red don't hardly matter. Some of us think you're making a mistake. We appeal to you, sir, on behalf of those who were killed and can't appeal for themselves. Let's cut out his tongue and chop off his nose and leave him for the coyotes. The Apaches would get the message."

Captain Vance sighed. "In the first place, Private, this prisoner isn't ours to do with as we please. He's a prisoner of the U.S. Army, and as such the Army will decide his fate. In the second place, although I sympathize with your feelings, as I indicated before, I won't condone torture or summary execution. We're taking him back, and that's final."

Relief coursed through Clay, and he allowed himself to relax as the troopers went about their business. Three more had been slain when the horses were stolen, and those three were now laid out beside the five other corpses and wrapped in blankets. Many an angry glance was cast at Clay as the soldiers worked, but no one else made bold to question the officer's decision.

In due course the troopers turned in, except for a pair of sentries. Captain Vance and Sergeant Conover sat talking over cups of coffee, and Clay could hear every word said. They talked of their military careers, and how glad both of them would be when they were assigned elsewhere. Both dreaded the Apaches and considered them the most savage tribe in existence.

Clay drifted off to sleep, although his dreams were dark and disturbing, of gallows and firing squads and of a vast throng shouting his name over and over while pointing accusing fingers at him. He awoke with a start, covered with sweat, and realized he had shifted closer to the fire. Bracing his elbows under him, he worked his body a few inches to the right.

Boots crunched on the ground. Clay looked up into the face of one of the sentries, none other than Private Williams. The trooper fingered the hilt of his knife and sneered. Apparently annoyed that Clay showed no fear, he kicked dirt on Clay and stalked off.

The eastern sky was brightening. Not much, but enough to indicate daybreak wasn't far off. Clay wished he could stretch, but his legs and arms were bound so securely he could hardly move a muscle.

None of the cavalrymen had thought to offer Clay a drink or a bite to eat after his capture, nor did they do so as they gathered for coffee and small portions of hardtack. Some wanted to partake of their rations of salt pork and dried beans, but Captain Vance wisely noted that they had many miles to travel on foot so they must use their rations sparingly.

After the meal a burial detail was organized for the slain troopers. The officer spoke a few words over the long line of earthen mounds; then his men formed into pairs and the long march began. Since they had to travel light, only essentials were taken. All of their saddles and blankets and many of their supplies had to be abandoned.

Clay had a rope looped around his neck and was led along by Private Norris. Private Williams walked right behind Clay, which gave Clay an itch between the shoulder blades. He didn't trust Williams not to thrust that knife into his back if the whim struck, so he kept a wary eye on the bloodthirsty soldier throughout the morning.

Toward noon Captain Vance called a halt in a gulch shaded on one side by a high rock wall. The men were allowed 15 minutes to rest. No one bothered with Clay, and as he sat there surveying the gulch he was stunned to see a swarthy face peering at him from behind a bush perched on top of the high wall. He blinked, figuring he was mistaken, and when he looked again, the face was gone.

Once the patrol was on the move, Clay stayed alert for any sign of the Apaches. After an hour had gone by and he hadn't seen hide or hair of them, he assumed his eyes had been playing tricks on him. There was no reason, after all, for the Apaches to risk their lives to free him. Most of them hadn't even liked him. They were probably glad he was gone, and by now were halfway to the Dragoons with their stolen herd.

About the middle of the afternoon Clay noticed something that gave him food for thought. All the troopers were plodding wearily along, their uniforms soaked with perspiration, their carbines held so loosely that a child could have knocked the guns out of their hands. He, on the other hand, hardly felt the heat. His wrists were sore from the rope binding him, but otherwise he was fit and filled with energy. There had been a time, not very long ago, when he would have been in the same condition as the soldiers. Had he changed so much in such a short time?

Evening came. By a sheer fluke the patrol stumbled on a spring. Captain Vance sent out six troopers in pairs after game and two of the soldiers shot jackrabbits. They used the only large container they had brought along, the coffeepot, to concoct a tasty stew.

The troopers had all eaten small portions. Captain Vance brought Clay the tiny amount left and a tin cup of water. "You must be hungry after all this time," the officer said as he set the food down. "It wouldn't do to have you starve to death."

Sergeant Conover, on seeing his superior go over to Clay, had drawn near and draped a hand on his revolver. "Be careful, sir. I was watching him today, and he's more Apache than I figured. Let him loose and he's liable to jump you."

"Then I'm counting on you to pull him off," the officer said, moving around behind Clay. He made short shrift of the knots and stood.

Clay didn't need an engraved invitation. He was so famished he would have gulped the stew greedily had he not remembered Delgadito warning him once against that very thing. "When your belly is empty, eat slow," the Apache had said, "or your belly will ache for a long time." So he ate the stew slowly, savoring every morsel, and never had simple stew tasted so delicious. He sipped the water afterward, and when he was done he pushed the cup toward the officer, who had sat observing him the whole time.

"I wish you spoke English," Vance remarked. "I bet there's a lot you could tell us about the Apaches and their ways."

"He wouldn't talk, sir," Conover said. "Not if he's been raised by them. He thinks of himself the same way full-blooded Apaches do, and they'd rather lose their tongues than betray their own kind."

"They are formidable enemies," Captain Vance conceded, "but they are people too, men like you and me. It's a pity our races couldn't have learned to live together in peace."

Forever after, Clay Taggart would be sorry that he hadn't gotten to know the officer a little better, and that he hadn't been able to do anything to spare the officer when the attack came.

Which it did, that night about midnight. Every last trooper was sound asleep other than the two guards, and one of them was dozing on his feet. Clay lay awake, staring at the myriad of stars and thinking how he would like to live his life if he had it to do all over again. Suddenly he heard a single footstep off in the darkness, and he glanced at the guards to see if they had heard too. Incredibly, neither had.

Clay slowly rolled onto his side so he could see the stretch of desert west of the camp. He studied the various cactuses and other plants, memorizing their vague silhouettes. Minutes went by, and one of the silhouettes changed its appearance. It happened quickly, so quickly Clay would have missed the change if he had blinked. Then he knew. The Apaches were coming for him.

Or were they? Clay wondered, as a disturbing thought intruded itself. What if the warriors out there weren't Delgadito's band? What if they were other Apaches, Apaches who would slay him as readily as they would the rest of the troopers? Actually, killing him would be easier for them because his wrists and ankles were bound. He was defenseless.

Clay bit his lower lip as he debated whether to call out and let the troopers know. He glanced at the nearest sentry just as a dark form seemed to rise up out of the very ground and envelop the sentry in shadowy tentacles. Noiselessly the sentry was dragged into the night and vanished behind some mesquite.

Twisting, Clay saw the second sentry suffer a similar fate. So swiftly did the Apaches pounce that neither man uttered so much as a sound. Clay looked at Captain Vance and thought of Vance's kindness. Impulsively he opened his mouth to cry a warning, but his shout was drowned out by the simultaneous blasting of five rifles. Gun flash after gun flash rent the gloom, and each shot scored.

Five troopers died in their sleep. Five more were shot dead as they scrambled from their blankets. Others were then hit as the Apaches fired at random. Bedlam reined in the camp, with soldiers yelling and cursing and firing every which way. Some hit fellow troopers.

Captain Vance was one of the few who kept his head. "Pick your targets!" he bellowed, racing among his men with his revolver in hand. "Don't panic! Stay low and don't waste ammo!"

Clay heard a slug thud into the earth inches from his head. More whizzed by above him. The deadly cross fire threatened to claim his life at any moment, and to save himself he tried wriggling eastward toward a forest of saguaro. He had covered a mere two yards when a fierce figure reared before him.

It was Private Williams, knife in hand. "You bastard!" he screamed, kicking Clay in the shoulder. "Your friends aren't saving you if I have anything to say about it!" His features twisted in fury, he lunged.

Clay saw the knife spearing at his face and frantically yanked his head back. The blade creased his chest, not deep but deep enough to draw blood. He rolled onto his side and coiled his legs in an attempt to kick at Williams, but the wily private skipped to the left, feinted, then slashed at Clay's throat. Clay whipped his body backwards, but he couldn't move far trussed as he was and the blade nicked him, searing pain through his neck.

"Hold still, damn you!" Williams hissed.

Clay was doing anything but. By pumping first one elbow and then the other he was able to scramble rearward. He was only delaying the inevitable, though, and both of them knew it. Williams wore a sneer as he advanced for the third time, and this time he wasn't going to rush his attack. His blade was held low, ready for the fatal stab.

Never had Clay been so totally, utterly helpless, and he wanted to shriek in fury at the fickle workings of deadly Fate. In a frenzy he kicked again and again, but Williams avoided his legs.

"First your throat, then your ears. I want to have them as keepsakes!"

All around them the battle waged, a one-sided battle in that although the troopers far outnumbered the Apaches, the Apaches had clear targets and the soldiers had none.

Clay hardly noticed. He was too busy trying to save his own hide. Private Williams abruptly took a long stride so as to get past Clay's legs and pounced, his knees slamming onto Clay's chest, flattening Clay under his weight.

"Now, you vermin!" Williams shouted, raising his weapon aloft. "This is for the others!"

Death stared Clay in the face, the same death under different guises that stares every man in the face sooner or later, and it was a measure of Clay's character that instead of flinching or cringing in fear he glared defiantly at the trooper poised to strike and responded with, "Go to hell, you mangy son of a bitch!"

Private Williams froze, shocked at hearing English. And in that instant when he was rigid, his forehead erupted in a gory geyser of blood, flesh, and bone.

Clay snapped his head to the right as the red shower peppered his face and hair. A drop landed

on the corner of his mouth and seeped between
his lips. He tasted blood, spat, and looked up to
see Williams crumpling slowly, as if the body was
no more than an oversized puppet that had had its
strings severed. Clay tried to shift, to throw Williams
off, but the private slumped across his chest, pinning
him in place.

Another figure appeared out of nowhere. It was
Delgadito, a smoking rifle in one hand, a pistol in
the other. He dropped to his knees, produced a knife,
and gave the private a shove. Swiftly he sliced the
ropes from Clay's arms and legs, and when Clay
sat up, he shoved the pistol into's Clay's hand
and pointed at the saguaro. Rising and wheeling,
Delgadito raced off into the thick of the conflict.

So much had happened so fast that Clay was hard
pressed to think straight as he rose and headed for
the vegetation. A harsh curse almost at his heels
stopped him, and he spun to find Captain Vance
rushing toward him with an upraised saber. "Don't!"
Clay blurted out.

The officer paid no heed. The saber cleaved the air,
nearly decapitating Clay. Again Vance swung. Clay
nimbly dodged, circled, and ducked a third blow.
Vance sprang, slashing madly, repeatedly, forcing
Clay backward, but there was nowhere Clay could
go that Vance couldn't follow. Instead of moving
closer to the cactus, Clay was being driven into
the swirling heart of the fight, increasing the odds
a bullet would find him. "Don't!" he said once more,
his final appeal. Whether Vance heard or not was
irrelevant, for the next second the saber swished
in an overhand swipe that would cut Clay from his
shoulder to his brisket.

Chapter Thirteen

Clay Taggart did what any man would do who craved life over the alternative. Thumb and finger worked in unison and the pistol banged twice.

Captain Vance reeled, tripped, and sprawled forward, the saber flying from his limp fingers to imbed itself in the dirt at Clay's feet. Clay grabbed the weapon without thinking and sped eastward, but he hadn't quite reached the saguaro when a strident scream made him look back.

Sergeant Conover and the remainder of the patrol were in tight formation, furiously working their carbines or revolvers while retreating northward. Shadows flitted around them, shadows that poured in withering fire. The troopers were resisting valiantly, but they stood no hope, no hope at all, of staying alive another five minutes.

Mentally cursing himself for being a jackass, Clay pivoted on a heel and ran to the nearest of the shadows. Delgadito sensed his presence and whirled, then they both dropped low.

"End it!" Clay bellowed in Apache.

Delgadito heard the words but was too astounded to react. It was unthinkable for Apaches to halt a fight when they had their enemies on the run and could wipe out every last one. Kill without being killed. That was the unwritten creed of his people, and here was a perfect opportunity to do so, to avenge themselves on the despised whites who had taken the land of their forefathers and forced their tribe into virtual slavery.

"End it!" Clay cried again. "For me!"

For no other person would Delgadito have done what he now did, and he did it not for Clay Taggart, but for Delgadito. He had learned from studying the rancher that Americans were always unduly grateful for small favors. It was a weakness he had exploited several times so far, and he did so again because the white man would mistake the act for yet another gesture of genuine friendship. Which suited Delgadito immensely.

Clay saw the warrior throw back his head and heard several piercing yips. As if by magic, the firing from the shadows instantly stopped. The retreating troopers continued to shoot wildly, though, for over a minute, until they were nearly out of sight in the mesquite. How many escaped Clay didn't know, but he guessed no more than half a dozen.

Specters flitted out of the night, four of them as grim as death incarnate. Fiero was first to speak, or rather growl, the question all four entertained.

"Why did you signal us to break off?"

"We could have slain them all," Ponce added.

Delgadito stood and stared after the fleeing soldiers. No one wanted to kill the Americans more than he did, but he had to make small sacrifices now in order to enjoy the fruits of his carefully formed plan later. One day soon he was not only going to be leader of a band, but war chief of the entire Chiricahua tribe.

"I too would like to know," Cuchillo Negro said.

Clay slowly stood. "Me ask Delgadito do it," he admitted, his nervousness making his Apache worse than usual.

"You?" Fiero responded, somehow contriving to make the single word an epithet unto itself.

Hostile glares were bestowed on Clay. They wanted an explanation, and the only one he had to give was that he didn't want any more troopers to die, that enough blood had been shed already. Yet confessing as much would only anger them further. So Clay kept the truth to himself and choose his words with care. "You picked me leader of raid. I made choice."

"The raid was over when we stole the horses!" Fiero declared. "White dog, you had no right to interfere! We will go after them and kill every last one."

"And the horses?" Clay asked.

"What about them?"

"Where one patrol, maybe other. They hear many shots, come quick. What then?"

Delgadito doubted there was another patrol within 50 miles, but he had to admit that White Apache had hit on the one thing that would give the others pause. The herd they'd gathered might mean the difference between life and starvation for dozens of their fellows in the months ahead. And too, such a successful raid would go a long way toward erasing the disgrace of Blue Cap's surprise attack. "I will do as White Apache wants," he announced. "After we take as many guns as we can carry."

Clay watched Delgadito move among the dead and examine their weapons. The rest of the warriors hesitated, then did likewise, each eager to claim his share of the spoils. Clay had no stomach for viewing the corpses, even if it was dark enough to conceal their ghastly wounds. He walked to a boulder and sat down.

What should he do next? Clay wondered. Stay with the Apaches or go his own way? Provided they'd let him, of course. There was still his score to settle with those who had wronged him, a vendetta he wasn't about to forsake short of being planted three feet under. Not while Gillett still had Lilly. *Clay's* Lilly.

A hand fell on Clay's shoulder and he jumped. Delgadito was holding the pair of matched Colts.

"I find these for you," the Apache said in English.

"I'm obliged." Clay checked the cylinders, found both fully loaded, and jammed the barrels under his breechclout. The Colts would come in mighty handy when he paid his respects to Gillett and the others. If only he could pay back those he owed without having to take any more innocent lives, like those of the soldiers! He stared northward and thought he saw dim shapes in the distance. Those troopers owed him their lives, owed the man they'd despised, and the irony was that they didn't even know it and likely never would.

Presently Delgadito returned bearing three rifles and cartridge belts. He nodded at Clay and trotted eastward. Clay dutifully followed.

Four sets of eyes watched them go with varying degrees of bitterness.

"I will never understand why Delgadito likes that white-eye so much." Fiero spat in disgust. "Remember my words. One day I will slit his pale throat."

"Not if I do it first," Ponce said.

Amarillo muttered something none of the rest could hear and trailed after Delgadito and White Apache.

Only Cuchillo Negro had nothing to say, although his thoughts were flying like the wind. Of them all, he suspected the truth. Of them all, he was the only one who would keep such knowledge secret. Delgadito was his friend and Cuchillo Negro would never betray that friendship.

Into the night the war party trotted until they came to a narrow, high-walled wash. The horses had been driven into a compact circle; then thorny brush had been piled to shoulder height on either side to keep the animals from straying. Now it was the work of moments to clear away the brush and mount.

Clay found himself on the zebra dun. To the thunder of pounding hoofs they galloped out of the wash and headed for the Dragoons. He felt the stiff breeze lash his hair and tingled to the rush of cool air on his skin. An exhilaration he had never experienced before made him lift his head to the heavens and yip like a coyote. To his delight, Delgadito answered, and the chorus was taken up by some of the others.

Clay Taggart was thrilled to be alive. For the moment he was at peace with himself and the Apaches. He was part of the band, heart and soul. For the moment he truly was the White Apache.

Epilogue

Be advised that a report has come to the attention of the Adjutant General's office which demands immediate attention. Two weeks ago this date a patrol was ambushed and almost wiped out west of the Dragoon Mountains. The five survivors have all given sworn testimony to the effect that a white man was part of the Apache band responsible. More details will be forthcoming shortly.

Headquarters regards this as a serious matter. It is imperative we ascertain whether this white man was taken captive at an early age and reared by Apaches or whether he has joined the Apaches of his own accord. Of special interest is whether or not he is part of the widespread criminal element known to

170

infest southern Arizona. A liaison between the two will not be tolerated.

Consequently, an order is hereby issued to the effect that every patrol, every trooper, is to be on the lookout for the individual in question. If possible, he is to be taken alive. If not, his body is to be taken to the nearest fort for identification.

Every officer in this command should consider himself formally directed to make the capture of this white Apache his first priority.

CHEYENNE

JUDD COLE

Born Indian, raised white, Touch the Sky swears he'll die a free man. Don't miss one exciting adventure as the young brave searches for a world he can call his own.

#1: Arrow Keeper.
__3312-7 $3.50 US/$4.50 CAN

#2: Death Chant.
__3337-2 $3.50 US/$4.50 CAN

#3: Renegade Justice.
__3385-2 $3.50 US/$4.50 CAN

#4: Vision Quest.
__3411-5 $3.50 US/$4.50 CAN

Judd Cole
Follow the adventures of Touch the Sky as he searches for a world he can call his own!

#5: Blood on the Plains. When one of Touch the Sky's white friends suddenly appears, he brings with him a murderous enemy—the rivermen who employ him are really greedy land-grabbers out to steal the Indian's hunting grounds. If the young brave cannot convince his tribe that they are in danger, the swindlers will soak the ground with innocent blood.
_3441-7 $3.50 US/$4.50 CAN

#6: Comanche Raid. When a band of Comanche attack Touch the Sky's tribe, the silence of the prairie is shattered by the cries of the dead and dying. If Touch the Sky and the Cheyenne braves can't fend off the vicious war party, they will be slaughtered like the mighty beasts of the plains.
_3478-6 $3.50 US/$4.50 CAN

#7: Comancheros. When a notorious slave trader captures their women and children, Touch the Sky and his brother warriors race to save them so their glorious past won't fade into a bleak and hopeless future.
_3496-4 $3.50 US/$4.50 CAN